About the author

Piers Anthony's five books – *Chthon, Sos the Rope, Omnivore, Macroscope* and *Prostho Plus* – have established him as a writer of great talent, on a par with the best of the new young generation of sf novelists. In an interview with the *Washington Post*, Arthur C. Clarke equated him with Delany and Algis Budrys. From the very first Mr. Anthony has been admired for his originality and inventiveness in both his serious sf tales and in his entertaining satirical novels.

Also by Piers Anthony and available from Sphere Books

MACROSCOPE

Prostho Plus

PIERS ANTHONY

SPHERE BOOKS LIMITED
30/32 Gray's Inn Road, London WC1X 8JL

First published in Great Britain by
Victor Gollancz Ltd 1971

Copyright © Piers A. D. Jacob 1971

First Sphere Books edition 1974

TRADE
MARK

Set in Linotype Juliana

Printed in Great Britain by
Hazell Watson & Viney Ltd
Aylesbury, Bucks

ISBN 0 7221 1175 4

PROSTHO PLUS

CHAPTER ONE

Dr. Dillingham was forty-one years old : a conservative, successful twentieth-century bachelor prosthodontist. His acquaintances thought him unimaginative; his patients thought he overcharged; his pretty assistant was secretly in love with him. He was, in short, a typical dentist with a secure future.

As pride goeth before a fall, so may the typical go before the atypical.

Dillingham was not pleased to see Mrs. Nostrand so early in the morning. She was overweight, her arches were fallen, her veins varicose, her manner insufferable. She seemed to be afflicted with most of the maladies imagined by man, with a single remarkable exception : she had virtually perfect teeth.

He wondered why she had chosen to inflict herself upon him. Possibly it was because every other dentist in the area had already informed her that however common prosthetic restorations might be, they were dictated by the requirements of health, not fashion.

'Mrs. Nostrand,' he began, knowing it was useless, 'no ethical practitioner is going to replace a healthy tooth with a substitute. Our purpose is to restore the mouth, as far as possible, to its original state of health. You should be gratified that you have no need of such service.'

'But all my friends have genuine gold inlays !'

Dillingham controlled his temper. 'I assure you, Mrs. Nostrand, they're not as good as nature's original dentin and enamel.'

'Mrs. Jones paid four thousand dollars for hers,' she said enviously.

He turned away to conceal his disgust. Had it come to

this? A running contest to see whose mouth could carry the most pointless wealth. . . .

'I'm sorry, Mrs. Nostrand,' he said with finality.

She stalked out, furious. He almost wished she *had* needed the work. It might have been easier to do it than to educate her.

Old Joe Krumpet, a too-regular client, was next. He was seventy and his teeth seemed to antedate the rest of his body : extremely old and worn.

''Nother blowout, Doc,' he said cheerily. 'Just put a patch on her and turn me loose.'

Dillingham looked into Joe's mouth. It was sheer carnage. He wondered how the man could stray one bite from a liquid diet. There was hardly a disaster in the manual his teeth hadn't succumbed to over the years.

'Joe, that tooth will have to come out. There isn't enough of the original structure left to make it functional, and further deterioration could affect your—'

'Nope. None of that fancy stuff. Just plug her up so she don't hurt no more. She'll las' as long as I do.'

He had a point there, unfortunately. Dillingham repaired the damage as well as he could, not even attempting to lecture the patient on oral hygiene. Joe Krumpet brought in his teeth for repair much as he would his vintage automobile. Who was a mere dentist to inject aesthetic complexities into his simple framework?

He finished with ten minutes to spare before the next appointment and retreated to his laboratory for a break. It was going to be one of those days : college kids who stuffed their mouths with sugar and looked blank at the mention of a toothbrush; businessmen who 'hadn't time' to undertake precautionary hygienic measures; women so afraid of pain that they screamed when he brushed a healthy tooth with the mirror. All of them carelessly throwing away the priceless

8

heritage of good teeth in their youth, heedless of the far more expensive and less comfortable substitutes necessitated in later life.

He was suddenly sick of it. Not of the work itself, but of the intolerable neglect he saw daily. So much of what he did would never be necessary if only people *cared*!

The radio was giving the routine details of another interplanetary space probe. Well, if there were other civilized creatures out there, surely they would long since have learned to preserve their natural assets! He visualized a baby bug-eyed monster smiling for the camera: 'Look ma – no cavities for six generations!' Assuming bug-eyed monsters had teeth. . . .

He rose and returned to the operatory, knowing that efficient Miss Galland would have the third patient properly prepared. At least he was spared the interminable details. Sure enough, there was a figure in the chair.

As pride before the fall—

Dillingham put on his professional smile, washed his hands, and plucked a bright metal scaler from the tray. This was a new patient, and—

He stared.

The face upon the headrest was an alien. It was humanoid, but only vaguely so. A great flat forehead dropped down to widely spaced yet narrow eyes, and the nose was a triple slit. The mouth was closed, set off oddly by thin purple lips.

Before he could substitute a more appropriate expression for the frozen smile on his own face, there was a noise. He looked up to see a second creature fiddling with the locking mechanism of the door. The humanoid must have been standing behind the panel, waiting for him to enter. The features were similar to those of the reclining creature, but all Dillingham noticed at the moment was the visible hand. It was grey, and the fingers appeared to be double-jointed.

9

Dillingham tried to think of a clever remark that would dispose of the situation, but his mind remained awkwardly blank. What conceivable explanation could account for . . . ?

'Gentlemen, there must be some mistake. I'm a dentist, not a plastic surgeon.'

Neither creature laughed. The one at the door straightened up and faced him silently.

Obviously he was the victim of an elaborate hoax. Nothing on Earth resembled these creatures. Someone at the local college must have set up this masquerade, fitting grotesque masks of that realistic flexible variety over their normal features. This was one of those disruptive pranks, funny only to the perpetrators. An initiation ritual. But how had they got past Miss Galland?

'Boys, I have a crowded schedule. Now that you've had your fun—'

The one in the chair opened his mouth.

Dillingham dropped the scaler to the floor. No mask could function as smoothly as this, yet the mouth was beyond credulity. The orifice was bone-dry and tongueless, and the teeth—

It was his business to know the normal and abnormal extremes of human oral anatomy. This far overreached them – but it was without doubt a genuinely functioning mouth, in a genuine functioning alien face. Since it was real, and no Earthly jaw contained dentures like these—

He decided not to ask questions whose answers might well be beyond his comprehension. This was no joke, and this was no longer a conventional problem. For some reason two aliens – extraterrestrial aliens, for all he knew – had come to his office to demand some service.

One sat expectantly in the chair. It could hardly be an accident. Why did anyone come to a dentist?

Somebody had a toothache.

The alien was not properly proportioned for the human recliner, but a few adjustments sufficed. Dillingham toyed with his instruments, wondering whether these creatures were dangerous. He couldn't afford to take a chance—

'Dr. Dillingham,' a voice called from the hall. The standing alien jumped, and something appeared in one hand. These two hadn't uttered a syllable so far, but they seemed to hear well enough.

'Dr. Dillingham!' the voice repeated more urgently, and the knob turned. It was Miss Galland. 'Are you in there? The door seems to be locked—'

The guard lifted his hand. He held a small object resembling a glass prism. He pointed it towards the door.

Dillingham didn't wait to find out what the prism was for. 'I'm busy at the moment,' he shouted, putting enough irritation into his voice so that she would realize it was important. 'Something has come up. Please reschedule my next appointment.'

Her soft heels retreated, and the alien lowered the prism. Perhaps there had been no danger – but it did seem best to keep the girl out of it until he could be sure. The aliens certainly seemed to mean business.

Did they use speech at all? The single glance he had had into the oral cavity gave him serious doubt that articulation as men knew it was possible. Still, there had to be some means of communication. . . .

Dillingham returned his attention to his patient. He seemed to be committed now, though of course he could not actually work on such a jaw. The mouth opened again and he surveyed it more thoroughly. It was a fascinating experience.

Four broad incisors lined the front section of the lower jaw, matched by five molars in the upper. This, at least, was what the teeth would have been called had they occupied a human mouth.

Biters opposed to grinders? Five to four?

What unearthly diet did this creature exist upon?

The overall problem of the alien presence became subordinate to the professional one. With dentition like this, how could he even guess at the normal state of the mouth? How would he detect the problem? And, granted a correct diagnosis, how could he ameliorate the condition? He knew nothing of the metabolism; he might kill the alien simply by applying a local anaesthetic. The creature might bleed to death from a single scratch – if it had blood. Nothing could be taken for granted.

The standing alien seemed impassive, but remained against the door, prism levelled. Suppose this were the captain of an alien vessel, and the patient a valued officer or crewman? It was convenient to think of these two as such, whatever the truth might be. Perhaps they had been on an exploratory cruise and had had difficulties that prevented an immediate return. Possibly their medical specialist had been incapacitated.

Whatever his reasons, the captain had seen fit to trust his man to the care of the nearest presumably competent specialist, rather than postpone the matter or handle it extemporaneously. The fact that the specialist happened to be of another world didn't seem to make enough difference to rule out the procedure.

There was food for thought here. Obviously the welfare of the individual was paramount, in the captain's society, surmounting even the formidable barriers between separate alien cultures. The individual who would trust a creature he had never seen before – an Earth dentist – to handle so precise and intimate a matter as the repair of an oral breakdown. . . .

That individual was either an absolute fool, or had enormous confidence in his control over the situation.

Dillingham glanced again at the captain. He did not have the aspect of a fool, and the prism glittered.

Yet the thing was impossible. The threat of a weapon could not create knowledge where none existed. It could not grant a human being the power to operate on alien metabolism.

The captain moved, gesturing with the prism. Dillingham immediately busied himself with the impossible.

The mouth was a paradox. There were no cuspids, no matched sets. Instead there were regular patterns of planed surfaces that could serve no conceivable masticatory purpose. The white units were obviously teeth of some kind, and firm pink gum tissue clothed the base of each unit, but the manner of the jaws application was a tantalizing riddle.

Dillingham felt as though he were in a surrealist dream. Despite the intricacies of their derivation – teeth had first been formed from modified scales of the lip, countless millions of years ago on Earth – he knew them to be straightforward tools. They were required for any creature who cut, tore, crushed or ground its food, unless it specialized into some substitute, as birds had. There was no point in having teeth at all unless they acted in one or more of these ways, and cynical Nature neither evolved nor maintained superfluous organs. This alien's teeth had to be functional, even if that function remained a riddle to the dentist.

How was he to define the problem? He saw no evidence of decay or abrasion. Every surface gleamed cleanly white. While he was hardly in a position to make an accurate diagnosis, all the evidence suggested health.

He tapped an incisor experimentally. It was solid. All the teeth were firm and without blemish. Why, then, had this patient come?

Dillingham set down his instruments and stood back. 'I

13

can't help you,' he said, trying to ignore the pointing prism and hoping his tone would put the message across.

The crewman closed his mouth, stood up, and went to the door. The captain handed over the prism and approached. Dillingham waited, uncertainly.

The captain took the chair and opened his mouth. Had they gone to all this trouble for a routine checkup?

Dillingham shrugged, washed his hands again, and brought out a sterile set of instruments. There didn't seem to be much he could do except oblige their whim. They *were* aliens, and it could be dangerous to cross them. He looked into the captain's mouth.

Suddenly it all came clear.

The crewman's mouth had been a healthy one. This mouth was not. The same peculiar pairings were present, the same oddly-angled occlusals – but several of the back teeth on the left side had badly ravaged lingual surfaces.

The visitors had anticipated one of his difficulties, so had shown him the healthy set first, as a model. Now he did have some idea what was wrong.

'Dr. Dillingham !'

The crewman whirled to aim the prism at Miss Galland's voice. Had half an hour passed so rapidly? 'Emergency !' Dillingham called to her. 'I'll be tied up all afternoon. Handle it as well as you can.'

'Yes, Doctor,' she replied with only the slightest hint of disapproval. His present procedure was at best highly irregular; with a real emergency, he should have brought her into the operatory to help. Miss Galland was a highly competent dental assistant, but he tended to use her more and more as a receptionist because she made a much better impression on recalcitrant patients than he did. She really deserved to see this astonishing set of teeth – but he still did not dare expose her to the mercies of such questionable aliens.

Meanwhile, he knew that the problems entailed by his unexplained cancellations would be tactfully handled.

He probed the first of the damaged teeth : the second bicuspid, for want of anything resembling a properly descriptive term. The captain jumped; no doubt about its sensitivity. It looked as though some potent acid had eaten into the surfaces and stripped away the enamel and much of the softer dentin beneath (again applying human terms to the unhuman). It had been a recent accident; there was no sign of subsidiary decay. But the present condition was obviously uncomfortable and probably quite painful, and certainly constituted a hazard to health.

Dillingham observed that the buccal surfaces had also been etched. Only an X-ray, that he could not risk on the alien flesh, could establish possible penetration of the pulp. This was a rough case.

It might be possible for him to repair the damage, or at least cover it with a protective cast – but only if he could anaesthetize the jaw. Novocain was out of the question; any drug might be fatal.

The whole thing was ridiculous. 'This is as far as I go,' Dillingham said firmly. 'I hate to leave you in pain, but my ignorance could kill you. I'm sorry.' He crossed his arms and stood back.

When they saw that he was not going to proceed, the crewman levelled the prism at him again. The Captain stopped that with a gesture. He stood up and recovered the instrument. He made sure he had Dillingham's attention, then aimed it at the wall and flicked a finger.

A spot appeared on the wall. Smoke curled up.

The captain made an adjustment and aimed again. This time a portion of the wall exploded, leaving a charred hole.

He returned it to the first setting and pointed it at Dillingham. The message was clear enough.

But what would be their reaction if he botched it? Should he violate his professional ethics under duress? Dillingham shook his head, sweating. Perhaps they were bluffing.

'Dr. Dillingham!'

Oh, no! Miss Galland had come back.

The captain nodded to the crewman, who whirled to unlock the door.

'Judy! Get away!'

'Doctor! What are you—'

Then the door was open and the crewman charged out. Judy Galland screamed.

Dillingham lunged at the captain, but the officer was ready. The beam from the prism stabbed savagely into his leg. Dillingham fell, clutching at the wound.

When the pain abated, he found Miss Galland standing beside him, her dark hair disarranged. The crewman had the prism again, and was covering them both.

'Doctor! Are you hurt?'

It was just like her to overlook the incredible in favour of the commonplace. She was not the fainting type, fortunately. He inspected his leg.

'Just a burn. It was set on low.' He stood up.

The captain resumed his seat. The crewman aimed the prism at the girl.

So much for resistance. The show would go on.

'I don't think they mean any harm, Doctor,' Miss Galland said. 'They must be desperate.' No hysterics from her; she had adapted to the situation far more readily than he.

Dillingham approached the patient. He had to quiet the shivering of his hand as he held a probe. Aliens, heat-beams – this was hardly the ordinary fare of a dentist.

But the problem of anaesthesia remained. Massive excavation would be required, and no patient could sit still for that without a deadened jaw. He studied the situation, perplexed, noting that the crewman had put away the prism.

The captain produced a small jar of greenish ointment. It seemed that this contingency had been anticipated. These creatures were not stupid.

Dillingham touched his finger to the substance. There was a slight prickly sensation, but nothing else. The captain gestured to his mouth.

Dillingham scooped out a fingerful and smeared it carefully along the gingival surfaces surrounding the affected teeth. The colour darkened.

The captain closed his mouth. 'How do they *chew*?' Miss Galland inquired, as though this were a routine operation. She had assumed her role of assistant naturally.

He shrugged. 'The moment they take their eyes off you, slip away. We can't be sure of their motives.'

She nodded as the captain reopened his mouth. 'I think they're doing just what *we* would do, if we had trouble on some other world.'

Dillingham refrained from inquiring just what type of literature she read during her off hours. He probed the raw surface that had been so sensitive before. No reaction.

So far, so good. He felt professional envy for the simplicity of the alien anaesthetic. Now that he was committed to the job, he would complete it as competently as he could. His ethical code had been bent by the aliens but not broken.

It was a full-scale challenge. He would have to replace the missing and damaged portions of the teeth with onlays, duplicating in gold as precisely as he could the planes and angles witnessed in the healthy set. While it would have helped immensely to know the rationale of this strange jaw, it was not essential. How many centuries had dentists operated by hit or miss, replacing losses with wooden teeth and faithfully duplicating malocclusals and irregularities? The best he could hope for would be fifty per cent efficiency – in whatever context it applied – yet if this stood up until the patient returned to his own world, it sufficed. There was no perfection.

Would a gold alloy react unfavourably with the alien system? He had to chance it. Gold was the best medium he had to work with, and another metal would be less effective and more risky. A good cobalt chromium alloy would be cheaper, but for really delicate work there was no substitute for gold.

He drilled and polished, adjusting to the old internal convolutions, while Miss Galland kept the water spray and vacuum in play. He shaped the healthy base of each tooth into a curve that offered the best foundation. He bored a deep hole into each for insertion of the stabilizing platinum-iridium pins. He made a hydrocolloid impression of the entire lower jaw, since the better part of the reconstruction would have to take place in the laboratory.

Both aliens started when he used the hydrocolloid, then relaxed uneasily. Evidently his prosthodontic technique differed from that of their own world.

'Sorry,' he said, as much to himself as to them. 'Since I am not familiar with your methods, I am constrained to rely upon my own. I can't rebuild a tooth by guesswork.'

'That's telling them,' Miss Galland agreed.

He needed a model of both sides of the jaw because it was bilaterally symmetrical. A mirror-image reproduction of the right side might reasonably do for the left. He ignored the upper jaw. He knew nothing of the proper interaction of these surfaces, so the opposing pattern could only confuse him. He didn't want human preconceptions to distort the alien pattern.

But his curiosity about the way those incredible teeth functioned was hard to suppress.

He worked loose the hardened cast. He applied a temporary layer of amalgam, so that the jaw would not be sensitive when the anaesthetic wore off. Then he had to explain to the aliens by means of pantomime that this was *not* the end product of his endeavours.

Miss Galland brought a plaster model of human dentures, and he pointed to the cut-away teeth and lifted out the mock reconstructions, then gestured towards the laboratory. After several repetitions the captain seemed to get the idea. Dillingham led the way, with captain, Miss Galland and crewman following in that order. The major portion of the job was coming up.

Patients seldom saw the lab. Few of them were aware of the enormous and precise labours that went into the simplest inlay, onlay or crown. This time, at least, he would have an attentive audience for his prosthodontic art.

Dillingham rinsed the impression immediately and immersed it in a two per cent solution of potassium sulphate while Miss Galland set up the equipment. There wasn't much else she could do, because special skill was required for the early stages.

The captain watched the routine with what Dillingham was sure was amazement. The aliens knew no more about the realities of dentistry than local people did! But what had they expected? Surely the techniques of North Nebula – to invent a home for the visitors – had points of similarity. Physical laws applied rigorously, whatever the language or culture.

He filled the impression with a commercial stone preparation, vibrated out the bubbles, and inserted the dowels and loops for individual handling of the teeth. While the die set, he simulated the remaining steps for the captain : the intricate wax mock-up of the onlay pattern for each tooth; the attachment of the sprue, so that the pattern and subsequent cast could be handled effectively; the investment, or formation of a durable impression around the wax pattern; burnout, to free the investment of wax and leave a clear mould for the liquid metal; casting (he didn't even try to explain about the problems of expansion and contraction of gold and cast): and finally the pickling, finishing and polishing of each unit.

The captain's eyes seemed glazed, though the procedures were elementary. Here in the lab Dillingham was master, whatever the larger situation.

At last he manipulated the hands of the wall clock to show how many hours would be required for all this. He assumed that if the Nebulites knew enough about Earth to locate a specialist when they needed one, they should have mastered local timekeeping conventions.

The captain was not happy. Had he thought that an onlay was the work of a few minutes? Probably, like most patients, he hadn't thought about it at all. Everybody *knew* dentists spaced out the time between appointments merely to boost their exorbitant prices! Ha (brother!) ha!

The captain produced what appeared to be a hard plastic rod and chewed it meditatively on his good side. Dillingham was afraid at first that it was another weapon, but saw that it was not. Well, every species doubtless had its vices and mannerisms, and this was certainly better than chewing tobacco or gobbling candy.

The patient passed the rod to the crewman, who glanced at it with interest but did not choose to add any toothmarks of his own. No conversation passed between them, but abruptly the captain left. The crewman took a seat and kept the prism ready.

Evidently they did not intend to leave the captives to their own devices while the onlay was in preparation.

'They don't miss any bets,' Miss Galland said ruefully.

Dillingham shrugged and bent to his work. It seemed that the surest way to get rid of the visitors was to complete the operation. He sawed his die into four separate segments, one for each damaged tooth, and plunged into the complex portion of the job. The wax he applied had to be shaped into the exact pattern of the desired cast. This, not the original tooth, was the actual model. The die determined the juncture with the living tooth, but the artistry lay in sculpting the upper surface of the wax into a serviceable and aesthetic duplicate of the healthy original.

He set the cruder plaster cast of the captain's jaw before him and began the most difficult construction of his career. It was not an image he had to make, but a *mirror image,* and his reflexes were hardly geared to it. Each of the four patterns would take several hours.

Night fell as he completed the second pattern. A new alien came to replace the crewman, but there was no chance to escape. They chewed sociably on rods, exchanged them, and parted.

'Dr. Dillingham!' Miss Galland exclaimed. 'That's how they talk! They make marks like that old-wedge-writing.'

It made sense. 'Cuneiform,' he agreed. That explained what the teeth were for! But the revelation, while satisfying intellectually, didn't help them to escape. The new guard was as vigilant as the first.

Night passed. Miss Galland slept on the emergency cot while Dillingham kept working. They both knew that help was unlikely to come, because the aliens had shown up on Friday and there would be no appointments for the weekend. Dillingham lived alone, and Miss Galland's room-mate happened to be on vacation. The captain had been quite lucky.

Something else occurred to him. 'Miss Galland!' She sat up sleepily. 'Since these creatures don't use sound to talk with, they probably don't associate it with communication at all!'

'Have you stayed up all night, Doctor?' she inquired solicitously. 'You must be tired.'

'Listen to me! We can plan our escape, and they won't realize what we're doing. If I can distract the guard's attention—'

She came alive. 'Now I follow you. We could have telephoned long ago, if . . . but how can we get him to—'

He explained. They worked it out in detail while he poured thick jel around the wax and vibrated the cup. She slowly opened the windows, then set up a chair in front of one and sat down. One agile flip could tumble her into the back lot – if the guard were off-guard.

The work continued. The guards changed again, and the new one did not realize that the window was open. Dillingham poured melted gold into the inverted hollows of the final mould. The alien's attention was taken up by the sight of the hot metal; he knew that was dangerous.

'Now,' Dillingham cried, as he plunged the hot cast into cold water. Steam puffed up, bringing the guard to his feet – and Miss Galland was gone.

Dillingham finished with a flourish. 'How's that for a set of castings!' he cried. 'Not to mention a slick escape,' he added as the guard turned to discover what had happened. 'The police will be here within half an hour.'

The alien had been tricked, but he was no fool. He wasted no time in a futile chase after the girl. He pointed the prism at Dillingham, fired one warning beam that blasted the wall beside him, and gestured towards the door.

Two blocks away they came to an overgrown lot. Hidden within the thick brush was a shining metal cylinder, large enough to hold several men.

'Now wait a minute!' Dillingham exclaimed as a port

swung open. But already he was coming to understand that the clever alien captain had anticipated this situation also, and had come prepared.

The cooling onlays burned his hand. Perhaps the aliens had never intended to let the Earth-dentist go. If they needed help once, why not again, during the long voyage in space? He had demonstrated his proficiency, and by his trick to free Miss Galland he had forfeited any claim to mercy they might have entertained. The captain meant to have his restorations, and the job would be finished even if it had to be done en route to—

The where? The North Nebula?

Dr. Dillingham, Earth's first spacefaring prosthodontist, was about to find out.

CHAPTER TWO

The Enen – for Dr. Dillingham preferred the acronym to 'North Nebula Humanoid Species' – rushed up and chewed out a message-stick with machine-like dispatch. He handed it to Dillingham and stood by anxiously.

This was an alien world, and he was alone among aliens, but this was his laboratory. He was master, in his restricted fashion, and the Enens treated him with flattering deference. In fact he felt more like king than captive.

He popped the stick into the hopper of the transcoder. 'Emergency,' the little speaker said. 'Only you can handle this, Doctor !'

'You'll have to be more specific, Holmes,' he said, and watched the transcoder type this on to another stick. Since the Enens had no spoken language, and he had not learned to decipher their tooth-dents visually, the transcoder was the vital link in communication.

The names he applied to the Enens were facetious. These galactics had no names in their own language, and comprehended his humour in this regard no more than had his patients on distant Earth. But at least they were industrious folk, and very clever at physical science. It was surprising that they were so backward in dentistry.

The Enen read the translation and put it between his teeth for a hurried footnote. It was amazing, Dillingham thought, how effectively they could flex their jaws for minute variations in depth and slant. Compared to this, the human jaw was a clumsy portcullis.

The message went back through the machine. 'It's a big toothache that no one can cure. You must come.'

'Oh, come now, Watson,' Dillingham said, deeply flattered. 'I've been training your dentists for several months now, and they're experienced and intelligent specialists. They know their maxillaries from their mandibulars. As a matter of fact, some of them are a good deal more adept now than I, except in the specific area of metallic restorations. Surely—'

But the Enen grabbed the stick before any more could be imprinted by the machine's chattering jaws. 'Doctor – this is an *alien*. It's the son of a high muck-a-muck of Gleep.' The terms, of course, were the ones he had programmed to indicate any ruling dignitary of any other planet. He wondered whether he would be well advised to substitute more serious designations before someone caught on. Tomorrow, perhaps, he would see about it. 'You, Doctor, are our only practising exodontist.'

Ah – now it was coming clear. He was a dentist from a far planet, ergo he must know all about off-world dentition. The Enen's naïve faith was touching. Well, if this were a job they could not handle, he could at least take a look at it. The 'alien' could hardly have stranger dentition than the Enens had themselves, and success might represent a handsome credit towards his eventual freedom. It would certainly be more challenging than drilling his afternoon class in Applications of Supercolloid.

'I'm pretty busy with that new group of trainees . . .' he said. This was merely a dodge to elicit more information, since the Enens tended to omit important details. Their notions of importance differed here and there from his own.

'The muck-a-muck has offered fifty pounds of frumpstiggle for this one service,' the Enen replied.

Dillingham whistled, and the transcoder dutifully printed the translation. Frumpstiggle was neither money nor merchandise. He had never been able to pin down exactly what it *was*, but for convenience he thought of it as worth its exact weight in gold : $35 per ounce, $560 per pound. The Enens did not employ money as such, but their avid barter for frumpstiggle seemed roughly equivalent. His commission on fifty pounds would amount to a handsome dividend, and would bring his return to Earth that much closer.

'Very well, Holmes. Bring in the patient.'

The Enen became agitated. 'The high muck-a-muck's family can't leave the planet. You must go to Gleep.'

He had half expected something of this sort. The Enens gallivanted from planet to planet and system to system with dismaying nonchalance. Dillingham had not yet become accustomed to the several ways in which they far excelled Earth technology, nor to the abrupt manner of their transactions. True, he owed his presence here to an oral injury of one of their space captains, who had simply walked into the nearest dental office for service, liked what he found, and brought the dentist home. But there was a difference between *knowing* and *accepting*.

Dillingham was in effect the property of the Enens – he who had dreamed only of conventional retirement in Florida. He was no intrepid spaceman, no seeker of fortune, and would never have chosen such unsettling galactic intercourse. But now that the choice had been made for him—

'I'll pack my bag,' he said.

Gleep turned out to be a water world. The ship splashed down beside a floating way station, and they were transferred to a tank-like amphibian vehicle. It rolled into the tossing ocean and paddled along somewhat below the surface.

Dillingham had read somewhere that intelligent life could not evolve in water, because of the inhibiting effect of the liquid medium upon the motion of specialized appendages. Certainly the fish of Earth had never amounted to much.

How could primitive swimmers hope to engage in interstellar commerce?

Evidently that particular theory was erroneous, elsewhere in the galaxy. Still, he wondered just how the Gleeps had circumvented the rapid-motion barrier. Did they live in domes under the ocean?

He hoped the patient would not prove to be too alien. Presumably it had teeth – but that might be the least of the problems. Fortunately he could draw on whatever knowledge the Enens had, and he had also made sure to bring along a second transcoder keyed to Gleep. It was awkward to carry two machines, but too much could be lost in retranslation if he had to get the Gleep complaints relayed through the Enens.

A monstrous fish-shape loomed beyond the porthole. The thing spied the sub, advanced, and oped a cavernous maw. 'Look out!' Dillingham yelled.

The Enen glanced indifferently at the message-stick and chomped a casual reply. 'Everything is in order, Doctor.'

'But a leviathan is about to engulf us!'

'Naturally. That's a Gleep.'

Dillingham stared out, stunned. No wonder the citizens couldn't leave the planet! It was a matter of physics, not social convention.

The vessel was already inside the colossal mouth, and the jaws were closing. 'You – you mean this is the *patient*?' But he already had his answer. Damn those little details the Enens forgot to mention. A whale!

The mouth was shut now and the headlight of the sub revealed encompassing mountains of flexing flesh. The treads touched land – probably the tongue – and took hold. A minute's climb brought them into a great domed air chamber.

They halted beside what reminded him of the white cliffs of Dover. The hatch sprang open and the Enens piled out.

None of them seemed concerned about the possibility that the creature might involuntarily swallow, so Dillingham put that notion as far from his mind as he was able.

'This is the tooth,' the Enen's message said. The driver consulted a map and pointed to a solid marble boulder.

Dillingham contemplated it with awe. The tooth stood about twelve feet high, counting only the distance it projected from the spongy gingival tissue. Much more would be below, of course.

'I see,' he said, able to think of nothing more pertinent at the moment. He looked at the bag in his hand, that contained an assortment of needle-pointed probes, several ounces of instant amalgam, and sundry additional staples. In the sub was a portable drill with a heavy-duty needle attachment that could excavate a cavity a full inch deep.

Well, they *had* described it as a 'big' toothache. He just hadn't been alert.

The Enens brought forth a light extensible ladder and leaned it against the tooth. They set his drill and transcoders beside it. 'Summon us when you're finished,' their parting message said.

Dillingham felt automatically for the electronic signal in his pocket. If he lost that, he might *never* get out of here! By the time he was satisfied, the amphibian was gone.

He was alone in the mouth of a monster.

Well, he'd been in awkward situations before. He tried once again to close his mind to the horrors that lurked about him and ascended the ladder, holding his lantern aloft.

The occlusal surface was about ten feet in diameter. It was slightly concave and worn smooth. In the centre was a dark trench about two feet wide and over a yard long. This was obviously the source of the irritation.

He walked over to it and looked down. A putrid stench sent him gasping back. Yes – this was the cavity! It seemed to range from a foot in depth at the edges to four feet in the centre.

'That,' he observed aloud, 'is a case of dental caries for the record book.' The English/Enen transcoder printed a stick. He turned it off, irritated.

Unfortunately, he had no record book. All he possessed was a useless bag of implements and a smarting nose. But there was nothing for it but to explore the magnitude of the decay. It probably extended literally within the pulp, so that the total infected area was considerably larger than that visible from above. What showed here was merely a vertical fissure, newly formed. He would have to check directly.

He forced himself to breath regularly, though his stomach danced in protest. He stepped down into the cavity.

The muck was ankle-deep and the miasma overpowering. He summoned the sick dregs of his willpower and squatted to poke into the bottom with one finger. Under the slime, the surface was like packed earth. He was probably still inches from the material of the living tooth; these were merely layers of crushed and spoiling food.

He recalled long-ago jokes about eating apple-compôte, pronouncing the word with an internal S. Compost. It was not a joke any more.

He located a dryer area and scuffed it with one shoe. Some dark flakes turned up, but nothing significant. He wound up and drove his toe into the wall as hard as he could.

There was a thunderous roar. He clapped his hands to his ears as the air pressure increased explosively. His foot slipped and he fell into the reeking centre-section of the trench.

An avalanche of muck descended on him. Above, hundreds of tons of flesh and bone and gristle crashed down imperiously, seemingly ready to crush every particle of matter within its compass into further compost.

The jaws were closing.

Dillingham found himself face down in sickening garbage, his ears ringing from the atmospheric compression and his body quivering from the mechanical one. The lantern, miraculously, was undamaged and bright, and his limbs were sound. He sat up, brushed some of the sludge from face and arms, and grabbed for the slippery light.

He was trapped between clenched jaws – inside the cavity.

Frantically he activated the signal. After an interminable period that he endured in mortal fear of suffocation, the ponderous upper jaw lifted. He scrambled out, dripping.

The bag of implements was now a thin layer of colour on the surface of the tooth. 'Perfect occlusal,' he murmured professionally, while shaking in reaction to the realization that his fall had narrowly saved him from a similar fate.

The ladder was gone. Anxious to remove himself from the dangerous biting surface as quickly as possible, he prepared to jump – and saw a gigantic mass of tentacles reaching for his portable drill near the base of the tooth. Each tentacle appeared to be thirty feet long, and as strong and sinuous as a python's tail.

The biting surface no longer seemed like such a bad place. Dillingham remained where he was and watched the drill being carried into the darkness of the mouth's centre.

In a few more minutes the amphibian vehicle appeared. The Enen driver emerged, chewed a stick, presented it. Dillingham reached for the transcoder – and discovered that it was the wrong one. All he had now was the Gleep interpreter.

Chagrined, he fiddled with it. At least he could set it to play back whatever the Gleep prince might have said. Perhaps there had been meaning in that roar. . . .

There had been. 'OUCH!' the machine exclaimed.

The next few hours were complicated. Dillingham now

had to speak to the Enens via the Gleep muck-a-muck (after the episode in the cavity, he regretted this nomenclature acutely), who had been summoned for a diagnostic conference. This was accomplished by setting up shop in the creature's communications department.

The compartment was actually an offshoot from the Gleep lung, deep inside the body. It was a huge internal air space with sensitive tentacles bunching from the walls. This was the manner in which the dominant species of this landless planet had developed fast-moving appendages whose manipulation led eventually to tools and intelligence. An entire technology had developed – *inside* the great bodies.

'So you see,' he said. 'I have to have an anaesthetic that will do the job, and canned air to breathe while I'm working, and a power drill that will handle up to an eighteen inch depth of rock. Also a sledgehammer and a dozen wedges. And a derrick and the following quantities of—' He went on to make a startling list of supplies.

The transcoder sprouted half a dozen tentacles as he talked and waved them in a dizzying semaphore. After a moment a group of the wall tentacles waved back. 'It shall be accomplished,' the muck-a-muck's reply came.

Dillingham wondered what visual signal had projected the 'ouch' back in the patient's mouth. Then it came to him: the tentacles that had absconded with his drill and perhaps fragments of his other transcoder were extensions of the creature's tongue! Naturally they talked.

'One other thing: while you're procuring my equipment, I'd like to see a diagram of the internal structure of your molars.'

'Structure?' The tentacles were agitated.

'The pattern of enamel, dentin and pulp, or whatever passes for it in your system. A schematic drawing would do nicely. Or a sagittal section showing both the nerves and the bony socket. That tooth is still quite sensitive, which means the nerve is alive. I wouldn't want to damage it unnecessarily.'

'We have no such diagrams.'

Dillingham was shocked. 'Don't you *know* the anatomy of your teeth? How have you repaired them before?'

'We have never had trouble with them before. We have no dentists. That is why we summoned you.'

He paced the living floor of the chamber, amazed. How was it possible for such intelligent and powerful creatures to remain so ignorant of matters vital to their well-being? Never had trouble before? That cavity had obviously been festering for many years.

Yet he had faced similar ignorance daily during his Earthly practice. 'I'll be working blind, in that case,' he said at last. 'You must understand that while I'll naturally do my best, I can not guarantee to save the tooth.'

'We understand,' the Gleep muck-a-muck replied contritely.

Back on the tooth (after a stern warning to Junior to keep those jaws apart no matter how uncomfortable things might become), equipped with face mask, respirator, elbow-length gloves and hip boots, Dillingham began the hardest labour of his life. It was not intellectually demanding or particularly intricate – just hard. He was vaporizing the contaminated walls of the cavity with the beam of a thirty-pound laser drill, and in half an hour his arms were dead tired.

There *was* lateral extension of the infection. He had to wedge himself into a rotting, diminishing cavern, wielding the beam at arm's length before him. He had to twist the generator sidewise to penetrate every branching side pocket, all the while frankly terrified lest the beam slip and touch part of his body. He was playing with fire – a fiery beam that could slice off his arm and puff it into vapour in one careless sweep.

At least, he thought sweatily, he wasn't going to have to use the sledgehammer here. When he ordered the drill he had expected a mechanical one similar to those pistons used to break up pavement on Earth. To the Gleep, however, a drill was a tapered laser beam. This was indeed far superior to what he had had in mind. Deadly but serendipitous.

Backbreaking hours later it was done. Sterile walls of dentin lined the cavity on every side. Yet this was only the beginning.

Dilligham, after a short nap right there in the now-aseptic cavity, roused himself to make careful measurements. He had to be certain that every alley was widest at the opening, and that none were too sharply twisted. Wherever the measurements were unsatisfactory, he drilled away healthy material until the desired configuration had been achieved. He also adjusted the beam for 'Polish' and wiped away the roughnesses.

He signalled the Enen sub and indicated by gestures that it was time for the tank of supercolloid. And he resolved that *next* time he stepped off-planet, he would bring a trunkful of spare transcoders. He had problems enough without translation difficulties! At least he had been able to make clear that they had to send a scout back to the home planet to pick up the bulk supplies.

Supercolloid was a substance developed by the ingenious Enens in response to his exorbitant specifications of several months before. He had once entertained the notion that if he were slightly unreasonable, they would ship him back to Earth. Instead they had met the specifications exactly and increased his assessed value because he was such a sophisticated practitioner. This neatly added years to his projected term of captivity. After that he became more careful. But the substance remained a prosthodontist's dream.

Supercolloid was a fluid stored under pressure that set rapidly when released. It held its shape indefinitely without measurable distortion, yet was as flexible as rubber. It was ideal for difficult impressions, since it could yield while being removed and spring immediately back to the proper shape. This saved time and reduced error. At 1300 degrees Fahrenheit it melted suddenly into the thin, transparent fluid again. This was its most important property.

Dillingham was about to make a very large cast. To begin the complex procedure, he had to fill every crevice of the cavity with colloid. Since the volume of the excavation came to forty cubic feet, and supercolloid weighed fifty pounds per cubic foot when set, he needed a good two thousand pounds.

A full ton – to fill a single cavity. 'Think big,' he told himself.

He set up the tank and hauled the long hose into the pit. Once more he crawled head-first into the lateral expansion, no longer requiring the face mask. He aimed the nozzle without fear and squirted the foamy green liquid into the farthest off-shoot, making certain that no air spaces remained. He backed off a few feet and filled the other crevices, but left the main section open.

In half an hour the lateral branch had been simplified considerably. It was now a deep, flat crack without off-shoots. Dillingham put away the nozzles and crawled in with selected knives and brushes. He cut away projecting colloid, leaving each filling flush with the main crevice wall, and painted purple fixative over each surface.

Satisfied at last, he trotted out the colloid hose again and started the pump. This time he opened the nozzle to full aperture and filled the main crevice, backing away as the foam threatened to engulf him. He certainly didn't want to become part of the filling! Soon all of the space was full. He smoothed the green wall facing the main cavity and painted it in the same manner as the off-shoots.

Now he was ready for the big one. So far he had used up about eight cubic feet of colloid, but the gaping centre pit would require over thirty feet. He removed the nozzle entirely and let the tank heave itself out.

'Turn it off!' he yelled to the Enen by the pump as green foam bulged gently over the rim. One ton of supercolloid filled the tooth, and he was ready to carve it down and insert the special plastic loop in the centre.

The foam continued to pump. 'I said TURN IT OFF!' he cried again. Then he remembered that he had no transcoder for Enen. They could not comprehend him.

He flipped the hose away from the filling and aimed it over the edge of the tooth. He had no way to cut off the flow himself, since he had removed the nozzle. There could not be much left in the tank.

A rivulet of green coursed down the tooth and over the pink gum tissue, travelling towards the squid-like tongue. The tentacles reached out, grasping the foam as it solidified. They soon became festooned in green.

Dillingham laughed – but not for long. There was a steam-whistle sigh followed by a violent tremor of the entire jaw. 'I'm going to . . . sneeze,' the Gleep transcoder said, sounding fuzzy. The colloid was interfering with the articulation of the tongue and triggering a reflex.

A sneeze! Suddenly Dillingham realized what that would mean to him and the Enen crew.

'Get under cover!' he shouted at the Enens below, again forgetting that they couldn't comprehend the warning. But they had already grasped the significance of the tremors, and were piling into the sub frantically.

'Hey – wait for me!' But he was too late. The air howled

past with the titanic intake of breath. There was a terrible pause.

Dillingham lunged for the mound of colloid and dug his fingers into the thickening substance. 'Keep your jaws apart!' he yelled at the Gleep, praying that it could still pick up the message. 'KEEP THEM OPEN!'

The sound of a tornado raged out of its throat. He buried his face in green as the hurricane struck, tearing mercilessly at his body. His arms were wrenched cruelly; his fingers ripped through the infirm colloid, slipping. . . .

The wind died, leaving him grasping at the edge of the tooth. He had survived it! The jaws had not closed.

He looked up. The upper molars hung only ten feet above, visible in the light from the charmed lamp hooked somehow to his foot.

He was past the point of reaction. 'Open, please,' he called in his best operative manner, willing the transcoder to be still in the vicinity. He peered over the edge.

There was no sign of the sub. The colloid tank, with its discharging hose, was also gone.

He took a walk across the neighbouring teeth, looking for whatever there was to see. He was appalled at the amount of decalcification and outright decay in evidence. This Gleep child would shortly be in pain again, unless substantial restorative work were done immediately.

But in a shallow cavity – one barely a foot deep – he found the transcoder, undamaged. 'It's an ill decalcification that bodes nobody good,' he murmured, retrieving it.

The amphibious sub reappeared and disgorged somewhat shaken passengers. Dillingham marched back over the rutted highway and joined them. But the question still nagged at his mind: how could the caries he had observed be reconciled with the muck-a-muck's undoubtedly sincere statement that there had never been dental trouble before? What had changed?

He carved the green surface into an appropriate pattern and carefully applied his fixative. He was ready for the next step.

Now the derrick was set up and brought into play. Dillingham guided its dangling hook into the eyelet embedded in the colloid and signalled the Enen operator to lift. The chain went taut; the mass of solidified foam eased grandly out of its socket and hung in the air, an oddly-shaped boulder.

He turned his attention to the big crevice-filling. He screwed in a corkscrew eyelet and arranged a pulley so that the derrick could act on it effectively. The purple fixative had prevented the surface of the main impression from attaching to that of the subsidiary one, just as it was also protecting the several small branches within.

There was no particular difficulty. In due course every segment of the colloid impression was marked and laid out in the makeshift laboratory he had set up near the waterline of the Gleep's mouth. They were ready for one more step.

The tank of prepared investment arrived. This, too, was a special composition. It remained fluid until triggered by an electric jolt, whereupon it solidified instantly. Once solid, it could not be affected by anything short of demolition by sledgehammer.

Dillingham pumped a quantity into a great temporary vat. He attached a plastic handle to the smallest impression, dipped it into the vat, withdrew it entirely covered by white batter and touched the electrode to it. He handed the abruptly solid object to the nearest Enen and took up the next.

Restorative procedure on Gleep differed somewhat from established Earthly technique. All it took was a little human imagination and a lot of Enen technology.

The octopus-tongue approached while he worked. It reached for him. 'Get out of here or I'll cram you into the burn-out furnace!' he snapped into the transcoder. The tongue retreated.

The major section was a problem. It barely fitted into the vat, and a solid foot of it projected over the top. He finally had the derrick lower it until it bumped bottom, then raise it a few inches and hold it steady. He passed out brushes, and he and the Enen crew went to work slopping the goo over the top and around the suspended hook.

He touched the electrode to the white monster. The derrick lifted the mass, letting the empty vat fall free. Yet another stage was done.

Two ovens were employed for the burn-out. Each was big enough for a man to stand within. They placed the ends of the plastic rods into special holders and managed to fit all of the smaller units into one oven, fastening them into place by means of a heat-resisting framework. The main chunk sat in the other oven, propped upside-down.

They sealed the ovens and set the thermostats for 2000 degrees. Dillingham lay down into the empty vat and slept.

Three hours later burn-out was over. Even supercolloid took time to melt completely when heated in a 1500 pound mass. But now the green liquid had been drained into reservoirs and sealed away, while the smaller quantities of melted plastic were allowed to collect in a disposal vat. The white investments were hollow shells, open only where the plastic rods had projected.

The casting was the most spectacular stage. Dillingham had decided to use gold, though worried that its high specific gravity would overbalance the Gleep jaw. It was impossible under present conditions to arrange for a goldplated, matching-density filling, and he was not familiar enough with other metals to be sure they could be adapted to his purpose. The expansion coefficient of his investment matched that of gold exactly, for example; anything else would solidify into the wrong size because of contraction while cooling.

Gold, at any rate, was nothing to the muck-a-muck. Gleeps refined it through their gills, extracting it from the surrounding water in any quantity required.

The crucible arrived: a self-propelled boiler-like affair. They piled hundred-pound ingots of precise gold alloy into the hopper, while the volcanic innards of the crucible rumbled and belched and melted everything to rich bright liquid.

A line of Enens carried the smaller investments, which were shaped inside exactly like the original impressions, to the spigot and held them with tongs while the fluid fortune poured in. These were carefully deposited in the vat, now filled with cold water.

The last cast, of course, was the colossal vat-shaped one. This was simply propped up under the spigot while the tired crew kept feeding in ingots.

By the time this cast had been poured, twenty-four tons of gold had been used in all.

While the largest chunk was being hauled to the ocean inside the forepart of the mouth, Dillingham broke open the smaller investments and laid out the casts according to his chart of the cavity. He gave each a minimum of finishing; on so gross a scale, it could hardly make much difference.

The finished casts weighed more than twenty times as much as the original impressions had, and even the smallest ones were distinctly awkward to manoeuvre into place. He marked them, checked off their positions on his chart, and had the Enens ferry them up with the derrick. At the other end, he manhandled each into its proper place, verified its fit and position, and withdrew it to paint it with cement. No part of this filling could come loose in action.

Once again the branching cavern lost its projections, this time permanently, as each segment was secured and severed from its projecting sprue. He kept the sprues – the handles of gold, the shape of the original plastic handles – on until the end, because otherwise there would have been no purchase on the weighty casts. He had to retain some means to move them.

The derrick lowered the crevice-piece into the cavity. Two Enens pried it in with power crowbars. Dillingham stood by and squirted cement over the mass as it slid reluctantly into the hole.

It was necessary to attach a heavy weight to the derrick-hook and swing it repeatedly against the four-ton cast in order to tamp it in all the way.

At last it was time for the major assembly. Nineteen tons of gold descended slowly into the hole while they dumped quarts of liquid cement into a pool below. The cast touched bottom and settled into place, while the cement bubbled up around the edges and overflowed.

They danced a little jig on top of the finished filling – just to tamp it in properly, Dillingham told himself, for he considered himself to be too sedate to dance. He wished that a fraction of its value in Earth-terms could be credited to his account. The job was over.

'A commendable performance,' the high muck-a-muck said. 'My son is frisking about in his pen like a regular tadpole and eating well.'

Dillingham remembered what he had seen during the walk along the occlusal surfaces. 'I'm afraid he won't be frisking long. In another year or two he'll be feeling half a dozen other caries. Decay is rampant.'

'You mean this will happen again?' The tentacles waved so violently that the transcoder stuttered.

Dillingham decided to take the fish by the tail. 'Are you still trying to tell me that no member of your species has suffered dental caries before this time?'

'Never.'

This still did not make sense. 'Does your son's diet differ in any important respect from yours, or from that of other Gleep tads?'

'My son is a prince!'

'Meaning that he can eat whatever he wants, whether it is good for him or not?'

The Gleep paused. 'He gets so upset if he doesn't have his way. He's only a baby – hardly three centuries old.'

Dillingham was getting used to differing standards. 'Do you feed him delicacies – refined foods?'

'Naturally. Nothing but the best. I wish we had been able to afford such galactic imports when I was a tad!'

Dillingham sighed. 'Muck-a-muck, my people also had perfect teeth – until they began consuming sweets and overly refined foods. Then dental caries became the most common disease among them. You're going to have to curb your child's appetite.'

'I couldn't.' He could almost read the agitation of the tentacles without benefit of translation. 'Doctor, he'd throw a terrible tantrum.'

Dillingham had expected this reaction. He had encountered it many times on Earth. 'In that case, you'd better begin training a crew of dentists. Your son will require constant attention.'

'But we can't do such work ourselves. We have no suitable appendages, externally.'

'Import some dentists, then. You have no acceptable alternative.'

The creature signalled a sigh. 'You make a convincing case.' The tentacles relaxed while it considered. Suddenly they came alive again. 'Enen – it seems we need a permanent technician. Will you sell us this one?'

Dillingham gaped, horrified at the thought of all that garbage in the patient's jaw. Surely they couldn't—

'Sell him!' the Enen chief replied angrily. Dillingham wondered how he was able to understand the words, then realized that his transcoder was picking up the Gleep signals translated by the other machine. From Enen to Gleep to English, via paired instruments. Why hadn't he thought of that before?

'This is a human being,' the Enen continued indignantly. 'A member of an intelligent species dwelling far across the galaxy. He is the only exodontist in this entire sector of space, and a fine upstanding fellow at that. How dare you make such a crass suggestion!'

Bless him! Dillingham had always suspected that his hosts were basically creatures of principle.

'We're prepared to offer a full ton of superlative-grade frumpstiggle . . .' the muck-a-muck said enticingly.

'A full *ton*?' The Enens were aghast. Then recovering: 'True, the Earthman *has* taught us practically all he knows. We could probably get along without him now. . . .'

'Now wait a minute!' Dillingham shouted. But the bargaining continued unabated.

After all – what is the value of a man, compared to that of frumpstiggle?

DENTAL ASSISTANT / HYGIENIST / LIGHT BOOKKEEPING QUALIFIED EXPERIENCED UNATTACHED MUST TRAVEL.

Judy Galland read the strange ad again. It had not been placed by any agency she recognized, and there was no telephone number. Just an address in a black neighbourhood. It hardly looked promising – but she was desperate. She shrugged and caught a bus.

She concentrated on the ad as she rode, as though it had further secrets to yield. She was qualified: she was a capable dental assistant with three years' experience in the office of a good dentist, and she was also a hygienist. She knew that few girls were both, and many would not touch the clerical end of it at all. She was single and willing to travel across the world if need be. She was twenty-six years old and looked it. She got along well with people and seldom lost her temper.

So why couldn't she get a job?

The bus jolted heavily over a set of tracks, shaking her loose from this pointless line of thinking. She knew what her problem was: she had worked for Dr. Dillingham, and Dr. Dillingham had disappeared mysteriously. A construction worker might fall off a beam and get killed, and nobody blamed his co-workers. A big-game hunter might get eaten by the game, yet his bearers could find similar employment elsewhere. A politician might get removed from office for malfeasance, while his loyal staff stepped into better positions. But just let one small-town dentist vanish—

She shook her head. That was inaccurate too. It was her own fault: she had tried to tell the truth. Naturally no one had believed her story of weird aliens holding her captive while forcing Dr. Dillingham to work on their astonishing teeth. There had been no substantiating evidence except for the simple fact that he was gone without trace. Now the aura of that wild story hung about her, an albatross, killing any chance she might have had to find other employment in the profession. In this corner of the world, at any rate.

Had she claimed that a mobster had murdered the dentist and sunk him in concrete with shoes of water (or was it the other way round?) she might have been clear. But the truth had ruined her. Aliens from space? Lunacy!

The bus halted at the closest corner to the address. She

43

stepped down regretfully. This was an unfamiliar section of town, ill-kempt and menacing. Beer cans glittered amid the tall weeds of a vacant lot. Down the littered street a drunk spotted her and shambled nearer. The bus blasted its noxious gases at her and shoved off.

Only one structure approximated the address: a cylindrical building several storeys tall and pointed at the top. Its outer wall was shiny metal, and surprisingly modernistic for such a region. Yet the lot had not even been cleared, except for the narrow boardwalk leading to the entrance.

She started to turn back, then. There was something unsubtly wrong about this ad and this address. What possible use could these people have for an experienced dental assistant, etc?

But the reality of her situation turned her about again. The bus was gone, the drunk was almost upon her, she had barely three dollars in her purse and her resources beyond that were scant. She had either to take what offered, or throw away all her training and apply for unspecialized employment. She pictured herself making beds, scrubbing floors, babysitting. Suddenly the nameless ad seemed more promising.

She outwalked the drunk and knocked on the cylinderhouse door. This was a circular affair arranged to resemble a ship's porthole. Modern architecture never ran out of innovations! After a few seconds it opened, the metal lifting up and out, drawbridge fashion. She took a nervous breath though she was not the nervous type and entered a small bare antechamber.

'Name?' a voice said, startling her. For an instant she had fancied it was Dr. Dillingham speaking, but it was some kind of recorded answering service whose intonation just happened to resemble that familiar voice. Apparently she still was not to know who was her prospective employer.

She answered the routine questions automatically. That voice unnerved her, and enhanced her depression. She had of course never let him know, but her initial respect for Dr. Dillingham's technical and ethical finesse had over the months and years deepened into a considerable appreciation of the man himself, and even—

She became aware that the questions had ceased. An inner panel opened. 'You have been accepted, Miss Galland of Earth,' the recording said.

A figure stepped through the new doorway.

Judy was not the screaming type. She screamed.

CHAPTER THREE

Dr. Dillingham was not in a happy frame of mind. Weeks had passed since he had last seen the light of a sun, breathed unconfined atmosphere, or even walked on land. Now the monstrous sentient swimmer within which he dwelt had deprived him of his transcoder, so that he could no longer make known his complaints.

His compartment was comfortable enough, and no doubt the Gleeps thought that sufficient. It had been outfitted with a bed, a chair, a workbench, selected prosthodontic laboratory paraphernalia and a water-closet – but this did not make it any less a prison. He used his equipment to fashion articles of solid gold, but this was sorry entertainment. He had no company his own size and no journals to relax with.

In an hour he would have to begin the day's labour – a prospect no less appalling for all its familiarity.

There were sounds in the living hallway. A visitor? He jumped up and tidied his smock, anxious to meet whatever oddity might appear. He was sure it would not be human.

The noise stopped. There was a tap on his door.

'Come in!' he called, as much to exercise his voice as in any hope he could be understood. He would be lucky if the visitor could ever *hear* sounds in the human vocal range. The creatures of the galaxy were far removed from Earthly experience.

'Thank you, Doctor,' a cultured voice replied. 'So glad to find you at home.'

Dillingham controlled his surprise. This was probably a transcoder in operation. It was hardly credible that a galactic would happen to speak unaccented English. Unless, some-how, a live *man* had—

The door opened. A dinosaur stood without. Its great head hovered a dozen feet above its powerful webbed hind feet, and its smaller front feet were held before it a little like the attitude of a begging puppy. A muscular tail twitched behind. It wore a modest dinner jacket with a black bow tie.

Dillingham gaped. Such a thing was impossible! This was not Earth, past or present, and even if—

'I beg you pardon,' the dinosaur said. 'Were you expecting someone else?'

Dillingham relaxed abruptly. 'Oh, you're a Galactic. I should have known.'

'Would you prefer to have me call at another hour? I did not mean to disturb you inconveniently.'

'No, no! Don't go away,' Dillingham exclaimed. 'Come in, sit down – or whatever you do. I haven't seen a sapient face in three weeks. Not since I was incarcerated here. I mistook you for – never mind. So many crazy things have happened the past few months that I should be acclimatized by now.'

The creature settled on the floor and wrapped its tail around its feet. The flat-snouted head was still above Dillingham's level. 'Allow me to introduce myself, in that case. I am, if I may make a free rendition in your terms, a diplomat from Trachos. I was asked by the, er, high muck-a-muck of Gleep to talk with you, since there appears to be some misunderstanding. If there is any way I can help—'

Dillingham had adjusted almost automatically to the notion of conversing formally in English with a dinosaur, after the initial shock, but he did have questions. 'If you don't mind my asking – how is it you speak my language? Everyone else has to use the transcoder.'

'It is my profession, Doctor. As I said, I am a diplomat – a free-lance diplomat, if you will. I always master the dialect before attempting to deal with an alien. The muck-a-muck was considerate enough to loan me a transcoder coded to Gleep/Earth—'

So that was where his machine had gone! 'You went to all this trouble just to talk directly to me?' This was impressive.

'No trouble at all, Doctor, I assure you. My species, being less aggressive than most and of poor digital co-ordination,' here he held up webbed fingers, 'survived by talking rapidly. Thus we became natural diplomats, and language is our pleasure. But you seem nervous, Doctor. Am I abusing your vernacular?'

Dillingham was embarrassed. 'No, you speak like a native. But there are a number of different life forms on my planet, Earth, and by an odd coincidence you—' He broke off, unwilling to say it.

'I resemble one of your animals? Please do not be reticent, Doctor. I must confess that your own appearance corresponds to a certain mammalian strain on my own world, mortifying as it may be to say so.'

'Well, I *am* a mammal—'

'Really?' The creature drew his reptilian head close. 'Do you give live birth to your young? Do you suckle them? Hair on your body? You have a' – here he paused delicately – 'a fixed body temperature?'

Dillingham was taken aback by the implied appraisal. 'Some of these traits are, shall we say, implemented by the female of my species. But yes – these are typical qualities.'

The dinosaur shook his head. 'Strange. I did not realize that intelligence was possible in a true mammal. But in a galaxy the size of ours—'

'Then you actually are a – reptile? You lay eggs, are cold-blooded, have undifferentiated teeth?'

'Of course – with the same reservations you mentioned for yourself. I, being male, do not personally lay eggs, and actually my blood is not cold. It merely matches the temperature of my body, which in turn matches my surroundings, which you will agree is the sensible system. No offence.'

Dillingham smiled. 'Then I don't suppose it is any insult to you if I mention that you resemble one of the most notable reptiles in the history of my planet. It's extinct now, but we call it the duck-billed dinosaur. I can't remember the technical name.'

'Ah. Probably Trachodon. I surmised as much when I interpolated missing portions of your transcoder's vocabulary.'

'You were able to discover terms I don't even know myself?' Dillingham asked, a little uneasy.

'By no means. If your language were rational, this would be possible, naturally, but this is hardly the case. The technical names for your dinosaurs – Stegosaurus, Ornithomimus, Brontosaurus – these were all in the memory-storage of your transcoder. You must have provided them at some time.'

'But I don't remember any such thing! I may have run across the words in some college text, years ago, but—'

'Interesting. Are you subject to the trance-state? Perhaps you provided more information than you realized.'

Trance state! Dillingham began to wonder just how much the Enens, his first galactic 'hosts', had learned about him. If they had managed to drug or hypnotize him—

'Suddenly it occurs to me I've been a trifle naïve,' he told the trachodon. Then, oddly, he found himself pouring out all his complaints to this unusual but sympathetic acquaintance. '. . . and then I was put to work instructing classes in metallic restoratives, as though being abducted from Earth wasn't bad enough. The novelty wore off in a hurry. Then the Enens sold me to Gleep, and for the past three weeks I've been wallowing in the unbrushed mouth of the leviathan, shovelling sludge out of trenchlike cavities and pouring in solid gold because the muck-a-muck won't allow me to experiment with anything cheaper. I have to live in this adapted lung-compartment. Oh, the Gleep monarch treats me well enough – but I can't get used to the idea of never going outside, even if there is no land here to walk on. As for actually *living* inside a three hundred foot long sea creature, like a parasite . . . I can't even flush the water-closet without remembering that my refuse is being drained right back into the bloodstream of—'

'This is understandable,' the trachodon said. 'It occurs to me that you are not well situated here.'

'That occurred to *me* three weeks ago! But how do I get away? Every time I try to say something—'

'I see no problem. To a Gleep, there is no higher privilege than serving Gleepdom. When you express dissatisfaction with your lot, the muck-a-muck must assume that the transcoder has broken down. Indeed, speaking as an objective third party, I must say that your attitude is atypical.'

'You mean there are creatures who would actually *enjoy* scraping decomposition off twelve foot cusps, ten hours a day? Who don't mind isolation?'

'Certainly, assuming they were capable of handling the work. Absolute comfort, absolute security, limited responsibility – it can be a very tempting proposition.'

Hope blossomed. 'Could – could you arrange to have one of these creatures replace me here?'

'I could certainly inaugurate the proceedings, if that is what you really desire. But I must warn you : once you leave Gleep, it will be almost impossible for you to return. Few are granted a second chance.'

'The *first* chance has been quite sufficient. Tell the muck-a-muck there are lots of Enens who are trained for the work, or who can instruct other creatures in the principles. Tell him – well, you're the diplomat. You know what to say.'

'Of course. But where do you wish to go?'

'Home!'

'Your native planet is some distance away. I rather doubt that you possess the frump or the stiggle to finance the journey at this time, particularly since you would first have to purchase your own contract and attain independent status.'

Dillingham thought about it. While he hardly approved of the manner he had become 'property', he knew that galactic law recognized the validity of that status. Earth was not considered to be a civilized planet, and therefore had few rights. The theory was that a savage admitted to galactic culture owed a certain amount in return for the education he picked up just by associating with higher species. He had a long way to go before becoming his own man again. 'I'll go anywhere, so long as it's above water and in the open.'

'I could arrange transportation quite readily to Electrolus, where I happen to have my next assignment—'

'Does it have solid land and natural sunshine?'

'Yes, but—'

'Done!'

Two hours later Trach showed him aboard a ship anchored on the surface. It hardly seemed possible that he had obtained his release so readily, yet here he was, out of the belly of the whale. Trach was certainly efficient!

'This isn't an Enen ship,' Dillingham observed. 'Too small. Where's the crew?'

'There is no crew,' Trach said, closing the hatch.

Dillingham realized abruptly that he was alone with a dinosaur – really alone. 'But you said—'

Trach walked by, his breath smelling of midsummer hay. 'I'm going to Electrolus, and there is room for you aboard my ship, so I simplified the procedure by purchasing your contract myself. Wasn't that what you wanted?'

Dillingham was hardly sure. The trachadon stood twelve feet tall without stretching and had an alarmingly powerful construction. The ridiculous jacket and bow-tie could not conceal the impervious hide beneath, or the rippling reptilian musculature. When he spoke, the jaws parted to reveal a ferocious array of teeth . . . but not far enough to enable Dillingham to determine whether they were the implements of a herbivore or a carnivore.

'Take-off may be a trifle uncomfortable,' Trach said. 'Would you like me to strap you in?'

The spare couch had enormous metallic bands for up to six limbs. The fastenings were far too heavy for Dillingham to manipulate himself; they were shackles that would hold him helpless, once clamped. 'I – I'll try my luck without the straps,' he said.

'Fine. I never bother with them myself. Sometimes I get hungry in mid-manoeuvre, and they become inconvenient.'

Sometimes he got hungry . . . Dillingham wondered just what rights a contract granted the owner. Were the duck-bills carnivorous? He couldn't remember. He gripped his bag of tools tightly, wishing he had something more sturdy than a slender dental scaler. But of course Trach was friendly. He was a reputable diplomat. He said.

Trach braced his tail against the floor and manipulated controls. Suddenly there was a jolt that threw Dillingham to the floor. 'Just a little finicky when she's warming up,' the dinosaur remarked. 'One of these missions I'm going to lease a modern ship. This one is apt to spring a leak in space any time now.'

Dillingham sat down abruptly on the couch and gripped a strap. Leak in space !

Another jolt, and the ship was moving. Trach activated a

screen, and the grey waves of the Gleep ocean appeared, rushing past at an astonishing rate. Then they were airborne, and the waves gave way to dank clouds.

It became warm. 'Do you have any temperature control for this ship?' Dillingham inquired sweating. 'I think the speed is heating the – I mean, the atmospheric friction—'

'Oh, there is some variation. We're reaching for escape velocity, after all. On this planet, in your terms, that's about twenty thousand knots. Nothing to worry about.'

Dillingham winced as the metal flooring became hot. 'Well, I'm a fixed-temperature creature,' he reminded the dinosaur apologetically.

'Is this uncomfortable for you? I had forgotten.' Trach obligingly turned on a frigid blast of air. 'Good thing that device is operative now. Sometimes it gets stuck on HOT.'

Dillingham nodded, shivering, though the metal fastenings were still too hot to touch. He wondered how many other minor inconveniences this ship would produce. This was certainly a contrast to the precision equipment of the Enens.

The ship shuddered and bucked, catapulting him across the burning floor. 'That breaks us out of the atmosphere,' Trach said nonchalantly. 'Better stay on the couch, though. Sometimes it—'

The dinosaur turned as he spoke, spied Dillingham far removed from the couch, and leaped for him. The enormous webbed hands caught him before he could scramble to safety. 'Got you !' Trach grunted with satisfaction.

Dillingham opened his mouth to scream, knowing it to be a thoroughly useless and effeminate gesture but unable to think of anything better. There *had* been foul pla—

The ship seemed to turn inside out. There was a sickening wrench of . . . something that threatened to deposit his stomach inside his braincase. Then Dillingham found himself seated on Trach's soft underbelly, both of them jammed into a corner.

Trach snapped around, snake-like, and set him on his feet. 'I meant to warn you, Doctor. The shift into overdrive is sometimes a little sticky. I'm used to it, but you could have been hurt. Are you all right?'

'Yes,' Dillingham replied, unsettled.

'From here on it will be perfectly smooth,' Trach said. 'Once this tub makes it through the shift, she's safe – until the shift back. That won't be for a couple of days, your time. We can relax.'

Dillingham decided to take him at his word. 'Thank you for all your trouble.'

Trach touched a button on a complicated machine. 'You over-rate the service I performed,' he said modestly. 'Ordinarily I would be offered a fair commission for straightening out the Gleep problem. But I accepted your contract in lieu of that, and it's worth—'

'A ton of frumpstiggle.'

'Which is several times my normal fee. That is a credit my account sorely needs. If I had failed to give satisfaction—'

The machine spewed out a mass of green material resembling fresh cabbage leaves.

'So you weren't just being nice, helping me out?'

'Doctor, it is my business to be nice, and to get paid for it. Too often I'm never given the opportunity. We'll find some attractive disposition for your contract, maybe a semi-private practice on Electrolus similar to the one you had on Earth, and both of us will gain. May I offer you something to eat?'

'That's – food?' Dillingham eyed the armful of leaves.

'Greenchomp, in your idiom. It's the only sustenance my species can tolerate. But the synthesizer can be adjusted for other things – usually. What would you prefer?'

Dillingham contemplated the machine. 'I'm not hungry

at the moment,' he said. 'What did you mean about never being given the opportunity to be nice? If you're a diplomat—'

'Free-lance. That means I'm my own boss, but if I don't produce, I starve. I go from mission to mission, and I was doing well enough until recently. But now – well, if I don't make good on Electrolus, I'll be awkwardly near insolvency. I'll have to scratch to provision my ship for the next hop, and that means—'

'Don't tell me. Let me guess. That means you'll have to auction off my contract to the highest bidder.'

'Something like that. And I'm afraid they don't offer as much for compatible locations. There's always a fierce demand for doctors and dentists in the radium mines of Ra, because—'

'My curiosity just radiated away. Let's agree that your problem is my problem, and see if we can't solve it.'

'If only we could. But it baffles me.'

'You seemed to handle the Gleep affair readily enough. I'm no judge, of course, but if you know your job and work at it, I can't see why you should have any difficulties.' It was amazing how quickly they had got on intimate terms. The confirmation of Trach's leafy diet and the image of deadly radium mines might have contributed something, however.

'I agree. But somehow I haven't made the grade recently, except on Gleep.'

'Tell me about it,' Dillingham said. 'Believe me, I am exceedingly interested.'

Trach flexed his tail restlessly. 'Consider my last assignment. The planet of Bolt engaged me to set up formal relations with the world of Gulp and arrange for a cultural exchange. I mastered the difficult language of Gulp – it's a glottal dialect – and trained myself to be adept at every nuance of planetary etiquette before setting one webbed foot there. I rehearsed my ritual compliments industriously. I'm sure everything was correct – yet I never got to meet the representatives with whom I had to deal. Despite my numerous hints, their monarch did not see fit to provide me with the necessary appointments, and finally my lease expired with nothing accomplished. I had to forfeit the commission.' His tail slapped the deck in frustration. 'How can I be diplomatic when I'm not permitted to talk with my clients?'

Dillingham shared his host's confusion. 'Weren't advance arrangements made? Didn't they know what you were there for?'

'They knew. The arrangements were made – and cancelled after my arrival. They never told me why.'

'Maybe they changed their minds about the cultural exchange, and didn't want to admit it.'

'Then why did they hire another diplomat after I left, an amphibian yet (!) and allow him to complete the entire programme?'

Why, indeed. 'That's typical? I mean, the same thing has happened on other planets?'

'Too many others. They just seem to lose interest, while other free-lancers make the reputation and commissions that should have gone to me. If I didn't know better, I'd suspect a conspiracy.'

'Do you know better? A situation like that—'

'That also is my business. I can spot corrupt politics as quickly as you can spot a rotten tooth.'

'But there must be some reason.' Dillingham tried to think of something plausible, but nothing occurred to him. 'Let's isolate the, er, area of infection. Exactly when did Gulp's attitude change?'

Trach considered. 'All the signals were positive at first. They sent an honour guard to meet me when I landed, and

I was provided with the most elegant accommodation. I interviewed the monarch the very next day. He was quite cordial, and I was sure success was in my grasp.'

'But—?'

'But nothing. That was the only appointment I had. They left me alone, and put me off when I tried to inquire. I know the brush-off when I get hit over the snout with it.'

'But are you *sure* there was no—'

'There was no foul play. No animosity. They simply changed their minds, and wouldn't tell me why. Most frustrating, for a professional.'

Something clicked at last in Dillingham's mind. 'May I have a look at your teeth?'

'My teeth?' Trach was surprised, but did not remark on the apparent change of subject. 'I have no trouble with them. When one row wears down, another takes its place. Even decay presents no problem as you mammals know it. Any damaged tooth falls out promptly and a new one grows.'

But he obliged the whim of the Earthman. Dillingham was astonished as he looked. Trach's flat bill contained myriads of proportionately tiny teeth. They extended in rows along the sides of his mouth, and extra teeth decorated the upper and lower palates.

'About two thousand,' Trach said. 'I'm not sure of the exact count because several rows have already worn away, and some haven't erupted yet.'

'You use all these just to chew greenchomp?' The stuff looked like cabbage, but he suspected it had the consistency of asbestos.

'As many as I need. We're herbivorous, like most civilized species.'

Dillingham let that pass. He'd have to try some of that greenchomp, assuming his feeble twenty-eight teeth could dent it. It was probably nutritious, and could hardly be worse than the pseudomeat extruded from modified Gleep sweat glands. Why an ocean creature had ever had to sweat—

He brought his mind back to the problem. 'How do you clean your teeth after a meal?'

'We employ a chemical mouthwash that dissolves vegetable matter in seconds,' Trach said. 'Though as I said, it doesn't really matter. Our teeth are—'

'May I see some of that?'

Trach was embarrassed. 'The synthesizer provides it also – but mine is on the blink in that area. I can't get it fixed until I return to Trachos. But that's merely an inconvenience. I could give you the formula—'

Dillingham nodded. 'More than an inconvenience, I'm afraid. You shouldn't go so long without cleaning your mouth.'

'But I told you it can't hurt my teeth. They—'

'That isn't precisely what I meant.'

'Oh? What *do* you mean?'

Dillingham was acutely embarrassed to sound so much like an Earthly TV commercial. 'Trach, you have halitosis.'

The dinosaur looked at him, perplexed. 'I don't understand.'

'You have BAD BREATH!'

'But my breathing is not affected. . . .'

Dillingham tried again. 'If I were a diplomat like you, I'd find some way, some gentle, discreet way, to tell you. As it is, all I can say is that your breath stinks of greenchomp. Particles of the stuff are wedged between your teeth. You have a lot of teeth, and it's pretty strong.'

'But greenchomp smells good. Does it bother you?'

'No. It's like freshly cut grass or curing hay. But then, I'm not a civilized, sensitive-nosed herbivore.'

'You mean—?'

'I mean. How does my breath smell to you?'

Trach sniffed. 'Faintly of carrion. But I'm accustomed to foreign stenches.'

'Right. You're a diplomat, so you've schooled yourself to ignore the crudities of the creatures you meet. But suppose you were a protected, royal-born creature, trained to notice the tiniest deviation from etiquette. Suppose your diet while herbivorous, did not happen to be greenchomp. Sup—'

Trach slammed his tail explosively against the floor, interrupting him. 'Suppose I met an alien who breathed sheer miasma into my delicate nostrils—'

'Yes. What would you say to him?'

'Nothing, of course. It wouldn't be—'

'Diplomatic?'

Trach paced the deck in a frenzy of mortification. 'How horrible? No wonder they wouldn't talk to me more than once. And worse – they may have assumed that *all* Trachodons smell that way. That I was typical. That would foul up every representative from my world.' He gnashed his teeth impressively.

'So maybe you'd better dash home and replace your synthesizer before going on to Electrolus?'

Trach slapped his webbed hands together. 'I can't. I'd have to admit my reason for delaying Electrolus. They'd never let me off-world again, after such a colossal blunder.'

'You're going to have to clean your mouth somehow, then, and thoroughly. The greenchomp must be removed. Unless the Electrolytes can't smell very well?'

'They can distinguish differing grades of clear glass – by odour. At twenty paces upwind.'

Dillingham sighed. The image of the radium mines loomed larger in his mind. 'I don't suppose you could get them to repair your synthesizer before—?'

'They're not mechanically inclined.'

The two lapsed into interstellar gloom.

Dillingham racked his brain for some solution to their mutual problem. It was ironic that a dentist couldn't come up with a simple way to clean teeth. The synthesizer, like so many of the ship's utilities, functioned erratically, and they were afraid to risk pushing it into a complete breakdown that would cut off even their greenchomp supply. Other chemicals besides Trach's original mouthwash might have done the job, but they were no easier to produce. Mechanical cleansing was also out of the question. A toothbrush – to clean two thousand teeth packed in like magnified sandpaper? Possibly a thorough scaling accompanied by copious rinsing with water would do the job – but it was obvious that this procedure would consume so much time, particularly as performed by Trach's webbed fingers, that the dinosaur would have to eat again before the job could be finished.

A blast of water from a pressure nozzle? Too splashy, and it still required time and care to get the wedged particles. Trach's skills were verbal, not manipulative – and what would he do at a public banquet?

What was needed was a simple but effective method to clean all the teeth in a few seconds. Agreed. But what?

'Is there any place you could obtain a temporary supply of your usual mouthwash? Enough to tide you over this one assignment?'

Trach twitched his tail reflectively. 'The dental university might have it in stock. But they'd be sure to make a report to Trachos, and—'

'Dental university?' Dillingham found himself interested for another reason. 'On a galactic scale?'

'Certainly. There's a university for every subject. Transportation, Communication, Medicine, Music, Dentistry—'

'Would this one – Dentistry – happen to have a school of Prosthodontics?'

'I'm sure it would. These universities are big outfits. Each one has a planet-grant, and students from all over the galaxy attend. Their standards are exceedingly strict – but there is no finer training. Graduates are set up for life. Had I been eligible to attend the University of Diplomacy—'

'Fascinating,' Dillingham whispered. He would have to think about this. Meanwhile the immediate problem remained: instant cleansing of two thousand teeth.

He thought of something. 'Trach, what can the synthesizer produce besides greenchomp? Without risking a breakdown, that is?'

'Oh, it turns out a number of mundane things. Several foodstuffs, yellow paint, mattress-stuffing, aromatic glue—'

'Mattress-stuffing?'

'For the acceleration couches. Sometimes they—'

'I see. How does it do on plastic foam?'

'I see no reason why it couldn't produce that. Of course the machine may not agree, but we can try.'

'Fine. I want soft foam that solidifies in two or three minutes to a firm but flexible texture. Non-toxic. Try for that.'

Trach obeyed, though there was obviously some question in his mind. After several tries he found a setting that produced a villainous purple goo that approximated the specifications.

'Now run a gallon of fresh foam and pack it into your mouth while it is soft. Chew on it a little, but don't swallow any.'

Trach was alarmed. 'In my *mouth*? What did I ever do to *you*? The stuff will harden—'

'It certainly will. Uh, you *can* breathe through your nose?'

Trach nodded dubiously. At Dillingham's insistence he

crammed the foam into his oral orifice. 'Tasheshts awrvul!' he muttered around the bubbles. 'Hwath a hway to dhye!'

'Now hold it there until it sets.'

'Urgh,' Trach agreed reluctantly. After a few minutes Dillingham gave the next instructions:

'Now open your mouth carefully . . . slowly – there. Now lift out the entire mass. Work it loose from the teeth – you may have to knock it a little – it's a foam impression, you see. A little harder. Oh – oh.' The cast seemed to have set some-what more securely than anticipated. Dillingham took his little prosthodontic mallet and tapped at the mass, finally dislodging it. 'See all that green stuff embedded it it?' he asked the dinosaur, pointing. 'That's the left-over green-chomp, all yanked out at once.'

Trach pointed in turn. 'See those little white bits also embedded? Those are teeth.'

'Oh.' He had forgotten how fragile the replaceable teeth were. No real harm had been done, but this was hardly a procedure that could be repeated several times a day. And he could still smell the green breath. 'I think I'd better think again.'

'Well, it was worth the try.' Trach opened a cabinet and withdrew a long-handled instrument. 'While you cogitate, I'm going to clean up the ship. We'll be approaching Electro-lus in a few hours.'

As the disc of the planet came into view on the screen, Dillingham still had no idea how to solve the problem. Idly he watched the dinosaur, a finicky housekeeper, running his cleaner over the control panel. A small attachment enabled him to get at even the daintiest knobs, and the grime vanished readily.

Suddenly the obvious occurred to him. 'Trach – is that an ultrasonic instrument?'

The dinosaur paused. 'Why yes. The handpiece operates at about 30,000 cycles per second, with a fine water spray. The cavitational action—'

'In other words,' Dillingham interrupted excitedly, 'the vibration is on an ultrasonic level, and causes microscopic bubbles in the water that burst and scrub off the surface quite effectively. On Earth we use a similar instrument for cleaning teeth.'

'For cleaning *teeth*?' Then Trach caught on. 'Why of course. I must have used this cleaner a thousand times, and on my most delicate equipment. I'm pretty handy with it, if I do say so myself. I could—'

'You could, with a few hours of instruction, become competent at dental prophylaxis, since you are thoroughly familiar with the mechanism. If you have clean tips you can use for oral work, and a mirror—'

'I can blast out every bit of left-over greenchomp! My breath will be pure, and – oh – oh!' He put aside the instrument, listening.

'It won't be easy the first few times, even so,' Dillingham warned. 'But at least—'

'Overdrive shiftback!' Trach cried. He leapt for Dillingham.

The ship turned inside out as they were dumped into the corner, but both were smiling.

'But I'm not a dentist!' Judy told the transcoder. 'I'm a dental assistant and hygienist and light book-keeper, as you must know.' The transcoder typed her words on to a stick in the form of indentations, and the North Nebulite took this. He poked it into the orifice beneath his triple-slit nose and chewed gently.

What jaw-motions constituted reading, as opposed to writing (typing?) she couldn't tell, and she was sure they could read by sight too. They had their own little ways of doing things. In a moment the creature fed the talk-stick back into the transcoder. 'You are Dr. Dillingham's assistant. Extremely competent but aloof. We searched for you. We obtained you. This is his laboratory. So assist.'

She peered around at the alien paraphernalia. It had been a substantial education, finding out exactly what had happened to Dillingham. Horrible as the purple-lipped, double-jointed North Nebulites – Enens, according to Dillingham's invented information coded into the machine – appeared, they were pleasant enough when understood. The two designated to show her around were Holmes and Watson, though either answered (or failed to answer) to either name. 'I never worked in the lab itself. Not that way. I can't make a reconstruction. I'm not allowed to perform dentistry on a patient – not by myself. I assist the dentist while he works. Where is Dr. Dillingham?'

Holmes assimilated the new stick and bit off a reply. The Enens had been cagey about late news on Dillingham, apart from vague assurances that he was doing well. She kept inserting the question in the hope that one of them would slip and give her an answer.

This time it worked. 'Dr. Dillingham? We sold him to the high muck-a-muck of Gleep.'

Judy started to laugh at the grotesque designation Dillingham had hung on that entity. He must have enjoyed himself hugely as he programmed the transcoder! On Earth he had always been serious.

She sobered abruptly. 'Sold him?'

'He was on contract, same as you. Hostage against the expense of his procurement and shipment. Perfectly regular.'

'I'm on—?! You advertised for a job, not a slave! You can't buy and sell human beings!'

'Why not?'

She was not the spluttering type. She spluttered. 'It just isn't done! Not on Earth.'

Both Enens masticated that. 'We aren't *on* Earth,' Holmes pointed out. 'Your ballbase players are bought and sold on Earth,' Watson said. 'Everything is in order according to Galactic codes,' they both said – or else the machine had choked over the pair of sticks and read the same message off twice.

'But Dr. Dillingham and I aren't ballbase – *baseball!* – players! And it isn't the same. This is kidnapping.'

The Enens nibbled sticks, not understanding what all the fuss was about. 'Everything is in order. We *told* you that. Now will you assist?'

Judy dropped that tack for the moment. The Enens had not mistreated her, after all, and it *was* rather exciting being on another world, and she could never have afforded passage on her own. At least she was on Dillingham's trail, and that alone just about made up for the rest of it. It wasn't as though she had had any particularly inviting future back on Earth.

'Well, how about letting me talk to the muck-a-muck? I can't accomplish much here by myself.'

'But you applied for a position at North Nebula!'

'I changed my mind.'

It took her several more days to establish that her mind, once changed, was absolutely set. She did convince them that their own technicians were far more competent in the laboratory than she, though far less competent than supposed at the time Dillingham had been sold. She suspected that Earth was about to sustain another dental raid, and she felt sorry for the innocent DDS that would be nabbed, but it was every ballbase player for himself. She was on her way to Gleep.

CHAPTER FOUR

'I am informed you are a tooth-healer,' the amorphous blob said. It spoke through a transcoder, since its natural mode of communication was via modulations in an internally generated electronic signal. The only way Dillingham could tell it was talking was by hearing the translation – which actually simplified things comfortably.

The creature was about four feet high and shaped like a rock when it came to a standstill. Its surface had the lustre of polished metal, yet it was flexible enough to make ambulation possible. There were no arms or legs; it seemed to move by wormlike undulations of its underside as well as the constant shifting of balance that brought about a controlled rolling.

'I am a dentist, yes,' Dillingham agreed. 'But I'm afraid neither my training nor my equipment would be of any benefit to you. My practical experience had been confined to—'

'We have verified your references,' the blob replied. 'If you would be of service, come.'

Verified his references ! Dillingham had not known he had any, on a galactic scale. This Electrolyte must have queried Trach and received a diplomatically optimistic report.

'You are asking me to look at – one of your people? I really don't know anything about—'

'We have made proper allowance for your appealing modesty. Come.'

That was Trach's handiwork, certainly. The dinosaur had entirely too much confidence in Dillingham's ability – or too vested an interest in the worth of Dillingham's contract.

Well, he was tired of idleness. He could at least accompany this creature, though any professional service was out of the question. Automatically he picked up his bag of equipment and the transcoder and followed the blob outside.

Electrolus was an interesting world, for persons who liked the type. The plants were crystalline and the animals metallic, with a metamorphic slant. Trach had said something about a silicon basis for life here, but the details had not been at all clear.

Trach had also arranged for a private duplex with appurtenances suitable to reptilian and mammalian needs. Dillingham was happy to share this with the diplomat. Trach might resemble a grade C nightmare out of Earth's past, but he was as familiar as a brother compared to some of the other galactic creatures encountered.

Although Dillingham's contract was a euphemism for slavery, he retained certain inalienable galactic rights: life, compatible environment, and the pursuit of liberty. The first was too often precarious and the second a matter of opinion, but the third vested him with a standard interstellar credit rating. His prior prosthodontic services had accrued normal commissions to his account, and even his transfer from one owner to another had added a percentage fixed by nebulactic law. He was handsomely solvent – but still a long way from the wealth required to purchase his own contract.

On Electrolus it was more than normally apparent that money – or frump or stiggle or whatever – wasn't everything. He could not enjoy the local cuisine: stewed silicate crystals hampered his digestion, no matter how succulent the grade. Trach's creaky synthesizer produced the only food available to him here – greenchomp, with constitution of leather and taste of hay. He could not enjoy the companionship of his own kind because he was, to the best of his knowledge, the only member of his species within a hundred light-years, or a thousand. He could not even relax with an informative text, since the Electrolytes had other, nonvisual, means of recording data.

He *could* admire the view, as he tramped after the serenely rolling blob. It was spectacular. The sunlight glinted and refracted and diffused amid the towering crystalline structures, kaleidoscoping colour. The entire countryside was jewel-like, with rising spires, steeples and minarets of brilliance along every azimuth.

Dillingham would have given almost anything for the sight of a green tree or a human face. He wondered what his former assistant, Miss Galland, was doing now, but cut off that speculation. A competent girl like her would have found another position immediately; even if he managed to return to Earth tomorrow, she would no longer be available.

Trach, at least, was fully absorbed in his business and didn't have to worry about homesickness. Every day he went forth to meet important personages and to arrange new liaisons, working diligently to solve whatever diplomatic problems Electrolus had hired him for. But Dillingham had no vital mission here. He had to wait, and hope that the dinosaur was successful, so that his own contract did not wind up in the tentacles of a radium mining foreman on Ra, or some even less enticing location. Lots of terrible places in the galaxy had standing offers for medical and dental specialists, because no one went there voluntarily. . . .

They had arrived. The native rolled into a gracious cave-like residence, and Dillingham accompanied it cautiously. He knew almost nothing about the custom of this culture, and could not guess how such featureless creatures had achieved space travel.

The occupant of the domicile greeted him with what he presumed was warmth: 'Contortions, O Toothman. Can you snog the dentifrice?'

Dillingham looked askance at his transcoder. It was supposed to render the alien signal-wave into intelligible English. If it went awry now, he would be in serious trouble.

'This, you understand, is the problem,' his guide said. 'Your instrument is not out of order.'

That was a relief. 'This appears to be a – a psychological matter. I certainly can't—'

'On the contrary, Doctor. It is a tooth matter. Our healers are baffled. The situation is getting out of hand. A number of our most prominent individuals, this one foremost among them, are baffled, yet nothing is done.'

'But I work on *teeth*, not speech problems!'

'Of course. That is why we hope you can help us. Anyone who can cure a Gleep toothache—'

Should he try to explain that dumping twenty tons of gold into the monster Gleep cavity in no way qualified him as a galactic psychiatrist? No doubt they would find the distinction plebian. Better a polite demurral.

He addressed the patient: 'Sir, I am not at all certain I can snog the dentifrice, but I return your contortions.'

The surface of the Electrolyte sparkled. 'Joy and rapturations! You clank the concordance!'

The guide rippled a lava-like furrow in Dillingham's direction and settled three inches. 'You comprehend him?'

'Well, not exactly – but I've had some experience recently with alien dialects. He was obviously wishing me well, and inquiring whether I could help him. My patients always say something like that, so I reply in kind.'

'I perceive your reputation was well-earned! Half of what he says is gibberish to us. It's frightful.'

Dillingham looked at the patient. 'Doesn't he mind this clinical discussion in his presence?'

'He can't understand us any more than we understand him. He's quite normal in most other respects, and healthy –

but he seems to be speaking another language. If only we knew what it was, we could programme a transcoder, but—'

Something jogged Dillingham's memory. 'Can he speak to the other afflicted Electrolytes?'

'No. They have even more trouble understanding each other. It's worse when they try to—'

'I suspected as much. I once had a patient on Earth who had asphasia.' He paused, wondering whether he should try to clarify that it had been the teeth he had worked on, not the asphasia. 'That's a kind of distortion of speech brought about by injury or disease. The patient thinks he's making sense, but the words are all confused. He has to learn the language all over again.'

'That's it!' the guide agreed. 'Truly, your cognizance is remarkable. Can you fix it quickly?'

What a living a huxter could make on this trusting planet! 'I'm afraid not. I know almost nothing about such aberrations among my *own* kind, let alone—'

'But surely, now that you have diagnosed it—'

Dillingham made one more attempt. 'I am neither a doctor nor a psychiatrist. I am a dentist. I repair teeth and try to restore the natural health of the mouth. What you need is someone who specializes in speech, or mental health.'

'Of course, Doctor. That is what our tooth healers do. How could it be otherwise?'

And in the past on Earth, barbers had practised medicine ... Would his refusal to consider the matter further be taken as a mortal insult that would prejudice Trach's diplomatic mission and lead to ... ?

Dillingham decided to have a look at the teeth. That much, at least, was theoretically within his competence. He hadn't yet observed any trace of a mouth, but that was minor.

'I shall try to snog the dentifrice,' he said matter-of-factly to the patient. 'Please open your mouth.'

The polish lost some of its lustre. 'Mooth?'

Oh-oh. Another missing word. 'Show me your tooth-container. Your oral aperture. Your—'

'Ah. My clank units.'

That made sense. 'Clank the concordance' might have meant 'speak the language'. The mouth would naturally be the speaking-place, the teeth the speech units.

'Right. I have to look at your clank units.' Then he addressed the guide: 'How do your teeth make speech?'

'They – talk. How else could it be?'

'But not quite the way mine do. You don't use sound. And surely the communication signal isn't generated directly by your teeth. It's electronic!'

'But isn't that the way everyone speaks?'

Ask a foolish question! The Electrolyte obviously had no conception of sound or vocal mechanisms.

But electronic teeth? He knew even less about electronics than he did about psychiatry.

Meanwhile the patient still hadn't got the idea, which might be a blessing. There was no mouth in evidence. 'Show me your dentifrice, please,' he said.

That was the formula. The upper section of the blob lifted, lidlike. Inside was a ceramic chamber with a dozen genuine, conventional teeth. They were arranged in opposing vertical semi-circles, and each was a sturdy molar adapted to the crushing and grinding of tough crystal.

'I see he has had some metal inlay operative dentistry.'

'What?'

Another point clarified. The average Electrolyte knew no more about prosthodontics than did the average Earthman. 'Some work done. Seems to be in order.'

'Oh. Yes, nothing but the best.'

Dillingham investigated more closely, reassured by the increasing familiarity of the orifice. His experienced eye traced the masticatory patterns and noted clues to the general health of the creature, though he knew he could not rely on such estimates when he knew so little of the native metabolism. Still, he saw no reason that these teeth should contribute to any general disorder. 'Gold inlays. Very nice work. But I note some corrosion.'

'Corrosion?' the patient inquired. Dillingham wondered how he could talk with his mouth wide open, then remembered that the speech was electronic. If it really were connected with the teeth. . . .

Circuits inside these molars? Perhaps a dentist *was* the person to consult about speech defects!

Such duality was not really more remarkable than that of the human apparatus. Take a mouth intended for mastication and salivation, pass air from the respiratory system through it, vibrate that air by interposing the cords intended by nature to seal off the lungs when under stress, and you had the basis of the human speech mechanism. None of it had been designed originally for communication, yet it functioned well enough. Why not teeth whose solid silicon structure became adapted to semi-conductor modulation?

On Earth there had been documented cases of radio reception via the metallic content of fillings in the teeth. Here, the natural currents resulting from stresses applied while chewing could eventually have been harnessed into broadcasting and receiving circuits. . . .

If only he knew more about such things! As it was, he knew that transistors were semi-conductor devices able to take the place of many electron tubes. This mouth could be the chassis of a radio set, each tooth performing a specific function in the circuit. Current low? Clench the teeth!

Which put the problem clearly beyond his competence. This was a case in which formal galactic training would be invaluable. Trach had mentioned a Galactic University of

Dentistry, but had stressed the difficulties of admittance: 'You have to have a high potential to begin with. They won't even consider you unless you are sponsored by an accredited planet. All the universities are like that. And few worlds will bother to sponsor an alien, when they have so many of their own people eager to make the attempt.'

'You'd advise me to forget it, then?' he had asked, disappointed.

Trach had agreed. How could an ignorant Earthman aspire to advanced training, when he couldn't even afford his own contract? Yet the dream wouldn't die. One of these planets he would make a bad mistake. If he wished to remain at large in the galaxy, he needed a galactic diploma.

Not that he wanted anything more than a prompt return to Earth. A secure practice at home. Certainly.

The Electrolytic teeth returned to focus. At least he could clean up the minor tarnish visible on the inlays. No risk there. The previous dentist must have been a trifle careless, for gold seldom tarnished unless there were impurities in the alloy. Apart from that, the work was expert.

He finished the polishing quickly. As for the language problem – there was nothing he could do about that. Under no circumstances would he drill into one of those fantastic teeth.

'Thank you,' the patient said. 'That tastes much better. What recompense may I offer you?'

The guide quivered. 'Your gibber – I mean, your aphasia. It's gone!'

'What do you mean, gone? You were the one who gabbled gibberish, sweetcore.'

The guide addressed Dillingham. 'O omniscient healer! You have cured my husband! How did you do it?'

Dillingham backed off. 'I didn't do it. I merely removed a little tarnish from his reconstructions.'

'You must have done something, Doctor,' the patient said. 'For weeks I've been trying to make my imperious wishes plain to this pebblehead, but she gave me increasingly unintelligible answers. My acquaintances have been even worse. It was as though they'd all blown their signal-coding teeth. But *you* understood readily enough, and somehow you brought them back to their senses. I really must reward you properly.'

'I assure you, I did not—'

'You replied to my salutation, and you eliminated the bad taste in my mouth, just as requested. An excellent job, not to mention this other inconvenience you alleviated.'

Discretion told him to let the matter ride, but something else overrode it. That little bit of polishing could not have affected the internal circuitry, and he could not accept credit for more than he had done. It was against professional ethics. The aphasia might return at any time, perhaps much worse than before, if the cause were neglected.

'You must stay for supper,' the husband said. 'It's such a relief to hear intelligible shunk again.'

There was a gasp (courtesy of the transcoder) from the wife. Dillingham saw his worst fear realized, and forestalled her comment the only way he could think of at the moment. 'Sir, may I check your teeth once more? While you were shunking I remembered a place I may have missed.'

'Certainly.' The great lid hinged up and the chunky teeth were exposed again.

Dillingham saw nothing new, but occupied time by re-polishing all the teeth carefully. He needed to think this out. H*a*d he done something that might affect the speech mechanism? Could mere tarnish somehow influence signal modulation? Tarnish was caused, in gold inlays, by electrochemical interaction of the saliva with impurities, but—

Full-blown, he had the answer.

74

'What were you saying, a moment ago?' he asked the Electrolyte. 'That it was a relief to—'

'A relief to hear intelligible speech again,' the patient replied promptly. 'After weeks of—'

The polishing *had* done it – and now he knew why. 'Sit down, both of you, please,' he said, knowing that the transcoder would provide the term for whatever they did in lieu of sitting. 'I have some serious news for you.'

Perplexed, they settled gently. 'What I have accomplished is only a temporary cure,' he continued in his more professional manner. 'The aphasia will inevitably return, unless you take immediate action.'

'Tell us what to do, Doctor,' the wife said anxiously, while the husband ran complacent ripples over his surface.

'First, I must make plain what has happened. Sir, when did you have all that gold installed in your teeth?'

'About six months ago.' Again, the transcoder was indulging in liberal paraphrase. 'It's a new technique, and very expensive – but I was tired of old-fashioned stone fillings that kept chipping away and falling out.'

'And your – problem – began several weeks ago. No – I know this is unpleasant, but I have to tell you that it was your speech that became unintelligible, not your wife's. Why else do you think she was able to communicate with other people, while you couldn't? Some of your words made sense, but others – well, you did say "shunk" instead of "speech" a moment ago, for example.'

'I did?'

'You did, dear,' the wife said firmly.

'And my handsome expensive prestigious restorations are the cause?' The Electrolyte wasn't stupid.

'Indirectly, yes. The work is very good – but all your metal inlays will have to be replaced with the old kind.'

In the next few minutes he made his case and left them

75

stricken. How much easier it would have been to avoid the truth! At times the dentist's duty, like the doctor's or tax-collector's was disturbing. But necessary.

Trach was waiting for him at the duplex. 'What have you got into, you hot-blooded mammal?' the towering duck-bill demanded. 'I have a complaint that you cured one of the leading citizens of the planet of his madness, then turned around and told him he'd have to remove all his costly fillings.'

'That's about it, I'm afraid.' News travelled rapidly, when every individual was his own broadcaster.

Trach slapped his solid green tail against the floor in exasperation. The sound was like a pistol shot – but how better to vent pique, than by banging one's tail resoundingly! 'Just when I had this planet's affairs sewed up!'

'I don't understand. Did my patient complain?'

'No. He's convinced you are a genius.'

'I'm duly complimented. But—'

'So he recommended to the ruling council, of which he is a member – temporarily on health-leave – that an immediate directive be issued forbidding the employment or retention of metallic restorations in any teeth on the planet. He has in-fluence. The directive has been published.'

'Already? In the time it took me to walk back here?'

'Already. And the league of local dentists is up in arms. They have some pretty potent backing of their own.'

'I see.' He saw. He had unwittingly provoked a political crisis. He should have consulted the local practitioners before making his recommendation. Naturally the dental league objected to having an outsider appear and demand that the latest advance be abolished. He'd feel the same way.

That was another reason he needed further training. There were always ramifications that extended beyond the strictly practical. How could he anticipate them all?

Trach paced the floor, his glossy reptilian skin flexing under the incongruous little dinner-jacket he affected. 'This means trouble. I don't like to say this, but it would be safer for both of us if you could see your way clear to retract your recommendation.'

'But it's an honest prosthodontic opinion. I—'

'This is no longer a prosthodontic matter.' Trach pursed his lips. He had extremely fleshy labia, necessary to articulate clearly around his twenty hundred teeth, and this expression was startling. 'I'm sure you know what you're doing, in your field – but diplomacy is *my* field, and I assure you that if we don't act soon, this will be a bad territory for tetrapods. This happens to be one of the few civilized planets where war is a recognized way to settle disputes.'

'War! You mean they'd—'

'Both sides are already enlisting mercenaries.'

Dillingham sat down, appalled. It was too late now to condemn himself for a meddler. He should have kept his opinions to himself until checking with Trach. 'What can I do?'

'Other than retract, you mean? You could meet with the dental league and explain your position. They might listen, if you catch them before hostilities formally commence.'

'I'll meet them! Is there much time?'

'Oh, yes. The first engagement isn't scheduled until this evening.'

'This evening! Let's not waste any time, then. I'd hate to have a war on my conscience.'

'Come with me.' Trach led the way with such assurance that Dillingham suspected this choice had been anticipated. The dinosaur didn't know much about dentistry, but he could manage people of any type.

'How do they do anything?' Dillingham inquired as they traversed the prismatic outdoors. 'These Electrolytes don't seem to have any hands, or any other way to manipulate objects. How can they feed themselves, let alone make war?'

'No problem. They employ remote-controlled devices for the manual tasks. Communication is the same as power, and it does economize on burdensome musculature.'

'Then aphasia must be a very serious problem, when it occurs. It would resemble paralysis.'

'Exactly. You can be a hero, if only you can pacify the league. But remember, you're dealing with conservatives.'

'Sure.' He reflected sombrely. It looked as though this were the brand of 'conservatism' that placed business interest ahead of cultural welfare. 'Can you offer any more advice, before I put my foot in it again?'

Trach could. This, too, had been anticipated. The next few minutes were an intensive briefing in diplomacy vis-à-vis Electrolus.

The representatives of the dental league were grouped like so many stones in their auditorium, ringed by spider-legged devices that were evidently their remote-controlled hands. Dillingham began to see why war was still sanctioned here; the destruction of a mobile unit might be inconvenient, but not fatal to the owner. Not so long as the mêlée was distant.

'You'll have to do the talking,' Trach said, handing him the transcoder. The machine had been turned off to ensure the privacy of their recent conversation. 'They won't accept your sincerity if I prompt you. They may ask me a question or two, but you'll have to convince them that your way is best. Otherwise—'

'I know,' Dillingham said unhappily. Outrage, war, the ruin of Trach's mission, and forced sale of Dillingham's contract for carfare home. He turned on the transcorder as he advanced to meet the dental league.

The spokesman wasted no time. 'For what purpose have you started this war, alien?'

Dillingham paused before replying, remembering Trach's caution against impetuous remarks. 'I think there has been a misunderstanding. I did not intend to start a war.' That should be imprecise enough. *They* were the ones who intended to do battle rather than admit responsibility for the aphasia, but they could save face by blaming it on him.

'Did you not directly and publicly contravene published League policy and conspire to set the governing council against us?'

'I am a stranger to this planet. I thought I was privately advising a patient of his best interests. I would gladly have left his care to you, had he not insisted on my attention.' And why *had* the patient sought an alien dentist, unless the local ones had already given up on him?

The pause that preceded the next question reassured him that his surmise had been correct. They were not going to challenge his right to minister to an awkward case – not when that line of investigation could turn so readily against them. 'Then you do not question League policy or practice?'

That was better. 'Of course not. I should hope the League has the best interests of the planet in mind.'

'Then you will retract your demand that all gold be removed from the teeth of our citizens?'

That was the sticky point. 'No.'

There was an angry flurry of sounds from the transcoder. Trach bowed his head, disappointed.

'That is,' Dillingham said carefully, 'I will not make such a retraction without the full consent of the League.' Trach's head popped up again hopefully, and the clamour faded. 'Since it was my careless utterance that precipitated this crisis, I feel it is best to obtain competent advice before making any further statements on the matter.'

Another pause. 'The advice – of the League?'

'Nothing less will do.'

The background discontent metamorphosed into background approval. Trach nodded unobtrusively. Dillingham was off the hook for the moment – if he didn't blunder again.

'A wise stipulation,' the spokesman said. 'What gave you the idea we might object?'

And so to the critical point. 'On my planet, the teeth are use principally for the mechanical reduction of the food, and only secondarily in connection with speech. Our teeth have no internal mechanisms – none, at least, of an electronic nature. Therefore our dentists think largely in terms of a single function: mastication. When I looked into this patient's mouth, that was what concerned me.'

'Astonishing,' the spokesman agreed.

'Then I discovered that you generate an electronic signal in your teeth, which is your means of communication. Because this is natural for you, and biological, you may not be aware of the precision required to modulate your signal so effectively, just as few human beings are aware of the sophistication of their own bodily adaptations. The fact is, the tiniest electro-magnetic interference in the immediate vicinity of your teeth can play havoc with your control, both broadcasting and receiving. The electrolytic action of the trace impurities in your gold alloy with the fluids of the mouth generates just enough current to tarnish the metal – and to distort the adjacent fields within the tooth. Thus the signal sent by a person with such a situation differs from that he intends. When this becomes severe enough to be noticeable, you have aphasia.'

He shook his head, glad they were listening (receiving) attentively. 'Possibly the field generated by the normal teeth is enough to start the surface erosion. Because the interference is external to the tooth, you will find no internal malfunction, which I know can be baffling. At any rate, because of your particular mode of communication, you can't afford metallic fillings until much more is known about this effect. That is why I recommended the removal of all gold from the teeth. Since aphasia is hardly my field, I should not have spoken prematurely. You have helped me to understand that.'

'But it is in our field,' the spokesman said somewhat condescendingly. 'We are concerned with the complete function of the teeth, though it had not occurred to us that trace tarnish would—' He stopped, unwilling to admit ignorance.

'We had a great many problems developing suitable metallic restoration on Earth,' Dillingham said. 'The work I inspected here was expert. I can appreciate your reluctance to – that is, I'm sure the expenditure of time—'

'We do not place convenience ahead of the welfare of the patient,' the spokesman said loftily.

'Then of course there is the expense. Gold is a rare and costly substance, and the waste involved in removing—'

'To hell with the expense!' the spokesman said. Dillingham glanced at his transcoder, startled. When had he programmed *that* vocabulary into it?

'Now if you'd like me to retract—'

Hubbub. Trach was maintaining a straight reptilian frown over a suppressed smile. The representatives of the dental league were suddenly aware that they had cut the ground out from under their own position. If he were to retract now, they would have to find some other way to treat aphasia, and that could be a lot more complicated than his solution. But if he didn't retract, they would lose face.

Trach came forward at this point. 'If I may make a suggestion, purely as a layman. . . .'

The Electrolytes were silent, and Trach proceeded. 'My charge's ignorance seems to have placed us all in a difficult situation. Perhaps, rather than require his apology, it would be preferable to banish him from the planet.'

Dillingham started. Whose side was the dinosaur on?

'This would reprimand him publicly for his mistake,' Trach continued blithely, 'while allowing the League a free decision in the matter of the gold. Perhaps the governing council would even be willing to make other concessions in order to avoid the necessity of rescinding their own hasty directive. Certainly this alien deserves punishment—'

'But he did mean well,' the spokesman said. 'The information about the aphasia is, er, valuable.'

Dillingham recognized the touch of the master. Trach had in one diplomatic motion converted the spokesman to the defence of the alien, while hinting at a profitable line of political attack. The League could allow the directive to stand as an extraordinary favour to the council, calling it an act of magnanimity instead of a humiliating reversal. The council would then be in debt to the league . . . an attractive prospect for the dentists, undoubtedly.

'Your attitude is certainly generous,' Trach said. 'Still, as owner of his contract, I feel responsible. This alien has caused you unpardonable embarrassment, and the least I can do is sell him to the mines.'

Oh-oh.

'The mines!' the spokesman exclaimed. 'We can't have that. He has done us a favour, really. We should purchase his contract from you, rather than—'

'But then you would have him on your hands, and he really shouldn't remain to—'

The spokesman pondered. 'True. We would much prefer to take it from here ourselves. His presence would be inconvenient, at best.'

'And the mines of Ra offer a very good price for dentists, since there is a chronic shortage.'

Dillingham's knees wobbled again. Was Trach determined to do him in?

The hubbub resumed. 'Because they don't *live* very long!' the spokesman said. 'No, it may be inconvenient, but we are not barbarians. We shall purchase his contract and abolish it, so he can go elsewhere.'

'He might not want to leave such a fair world as this,' Trach remarked, and once again Dillingham wished he'd quit while he was ahead. 'Though I suppose if you were to sponsor him for something time-consuming, such as further education—'

'The very thing. We can select a very complicated programme such as—'

'Such as the one at the Galactic University of Dentistry, School of Prosthodontistry,' Trach finished neatly. 'A most perceptive decision. I can, for a nominal fee, make the arrangements immediately.'

Dillingham almost fainted from surprise and relief. He had thought the friendly dinosaur had forgotten that conversation.

'Excellent,' the spokesman said, though it was evident that he had had a different programme in mind. 'Now that we have solved that problem, we can mmph the council and set about scrutchulating the hornswoggle.'

Trach looked quickly at Dillingham and held one webbed finger to his lips. Together they beat an inconspicuous retreat.

'But I'm *not* a dentist!' Judy told the muck-a-muck. 'I'm just looking for Dr. Dillingham, so I can – assist him.'

'He departed last week,' the whale-like ruler of waterworld Gleep communicated. This was the first time she had conversed with an entity while standing inside him, but such was galactic existence.

'Then I must follow him.'

'Do you realize that we paid a hundred pounds of premium-grade frumpstiggle for your contract? You were billed as an associate of Dr. Dillingham, the famous exodontist. Now the prince's molars are beginning to itch again, and only a practitioner of Dillingham's status can abate the condition.'

'If Dr. Dillingham made the restorations, those teeth should be giving no trouble,' she said loyally. 'Probably all your son needs now is some instruction in preventive maintenance. Teeth can't be ignored, you know; you have to take care of them.'

'That's exactly what *he* said! You *are* his associate!'

She sighed. 'In that respect, yes. But as for—'

'Excellent! Provide him with expert instruction.'

'First we have to come to an understanding,' she said. She was, by fits and starts, learning how to deal with galactics. 'If I instruct the prince, you must agree to send me to the planet that Dr. Dillingham went to.'

'Gladly. He travelled hence with a free-lance diplomat from Trachos. Their destination was – let me look it up in my tertiary memory bank – Electrolus.'

'Fine. I'll go there.' Then she reconsidered. 'I came to Enen too late, and to Gleep too late. How can I be sure he'll still be at Electrolus, when . . . ?'

The communications tentacles of the huge Gleep creature's lung chamber waved, and the transcoder dutifully rendered this visual signal into English. 'A perspicacious point. Suppose we send you to the diplomat's *following* client? That's – one moment, please – Ra. The radium exporter.'

She was dubious. 'But what if Dr. Dillingham stays at Electrolus after all?'

'Then at least you'll be in touch with Trach, the diplomat. He is an obliging fellow, and he has his own ship.'

She considered that, still not entirely satisfied. She had had experience with obliging fellows possessing their own transportation. Dillingham had been a pleasing contrast – so serious, so dedicated to his profession.

But of course this was not Earth, and it did seem to be her best chance. 'All right. Ra it is. Let's see the prince now.'

CHAPTER FIVE

He entered the booth when his turn came and waited somewhat apprehensively for it to perform. The panel behind shut him in and ground tight.

The interior was dark and unbearably hot, making sweat break out and stream down his body. Then the temperature dropped so precipitously that the moisture crystallized upon his skin and flaked away with the violence of his shivering. The air grew thick and bitter, then gaspingly rare. Light blazed, then faded into impenetrable black. A complete sonic spectrum of noise smote him, followed by crashing silence. His nose reacted to a gamut of irritation. He sneezed.

Abruptly it was spring on a clover hillside, waft of nectar and hum of bumble-bee. The air was refreshingly brisk. The booth had zeroed in on his metabolism.

'Identity?' a deceptively feminine voice inquired from nowhere, and a sign flashed with the word printed in italics. English.

'My name is Dillingham,' he said clearly, remembering his instructions. 'I am a male mammalian biped evolved on planet Earth. I am applying for admission to the School of Prosthodontics as an initiate of the appropriate level.'

After a pause the booth replied sweetly: 'Misinformation. You are a quadruped.'

'Correction,' Dillingham said quickly. 'I am *evolved* from quadruped.' He spread his hands and touched the wall. 'Technically tetrapod, anterior limbs no longer employed for locomotion. Digits posses sensitivity, dexterity—'

'Noted.' But before he could breathe relief, it had another

85

objection : 'Earth planet has not yet achieved galactic accreditation. Application invalid.'

'I have been sponsored by the Dental League of Electrolus,' he said. He saw already how far he would have got without that potent endorsement.

'Verified. Provisional application granted. Probability of acceptance after preliminary investigation : twenty-one per cent. Fee : Thirteen thousand, two hundred and five dollars, four cents, seven mills, payable immediately.'

'Agreed,' he said, appalled at both the machine's efficiency in adapting to his language and conventions, and the cost of application. He knew that the fee covered only the seventy hour investigation of his credentials; if finally admitted as a student, he would have to pay another fee of as much as a hundred thousand dollars for the first term. If rejected, he would get no rebate.

His sponsor, Electrolus, was paying for it, thanks to Trach's diplomatic footwork. If he failed to gain admission, there would be no consequence – except that his chance to really improve himself would be gone. He could never afford training at the University on his own, even if the sponsorship requirement should be waived.

Even so, he hoped that what the University had to offer was worth it. Over thirteen thousand dollars had already been drained from the Electrolus account here by his verbal agreement – for a twenty-one per cent probability of acceptance !

'Present your anterior limb, buccal surface forward.'

He put out his left hand again, deciding that 'buccal' in this context equated with the back of the hand. He was nervous in spite of the assurance he had been given that this process was harmless. A mist appeared around it, puffed and vanished, leaving an iridescent band clasped around, or perhaps bonded into, the skin of his wrist.

The opposite side of the booth opened and he stepped into a lighted corridor. He held up his hand and saw that the left of it was bright while the right was dull. This remained constant even when he twisted his wrist, the glow being independent of his motion. He proceeded left.

At the end of the passage was a row of elevators. Other creatures of diverse proportions moved towards these, guided by the glows on their appendages. His own led him to a particular unit. Its panel was open, and he entered.

The door was closed as he took hold of the supportive bars. The unit moved, not up or down as he had expected, but backwards. He clung desperately to the support as the fierce acceleration hurled him at the door.

There was something like a porthole in the side through which he could make out racing lights and darknesses. If these were stationary sources of contrast, his velocity was phenomenal. His stomach jumped as the vehicle dipped and tilted; then it plummeted down as though dropped from a cliff.

Dillingham was reminded of an amusement park he had visited as a child on Earth. There had been a ride through the dark something like this. He was sure that the transport system of the university had not been designed for thrills, however; it merely reflected the fact that there was a long way to go and many others in line. The elevators would not function at all for any creature not wearing proper identification. Established galactics took such things in stride without even noticing.

Finally the roller-coaster/elevator decelerated and stopped. The door opened and he stepped dizzily into his residence for the duration, suppressing incipient motion sickness.

The apartment was attractive enough. The air was sweet, the light moderate, the temperature comfortable. Earth-like vines decorated the trellises, and couches fit for bipeds were placed against the walls. In the centre of the main room stood a handsome but mysterious device.

Something emerged from an alcove. It was a creature resembling an oversized pincushion with legs, one of which sported the ubiquitous iridescent band. It honked.

'Greetings, room-mate,' a speaker from the central artifact said. Dillingham realized that it was a multiple-dialect translator.

'How do you do,' he said. The translator honked, and the pincushion came all the way into the room.

'I am from no equivalent term,' it said in tootles.

Dillingham hesitated to comment, until he realized that the confusion lay in the translation. There was no name in English for Pincushion's planet, since Earth knew little of galactic geography and nothing of interspecies commerce. 'Substitute "Pincushion" for the missing term,' he advised the machine, 'and make the same kind of adjustment for any terms that may not be renderable into Pincushion's dialect.' He turned to the creature. 'I am from Earth. I presume you are also here to make application for admittance to the School of Prosthodontics?'

The translator honked, once. Dillingham waited, but that was all.

Pincushion honked. 'Yes, of course. I'm sure all beings assigned to this dormitory are 1.0 gravity, oxygen-imbibing ambulators applying as students. The administration is very careful to group compatible species.'

Apparently a single honk could convey a paragraph. Perhaps there were frequencies he couldn't hear. Then again, it might be the inefficiency of his own tongue. 'I'm new to all this,' he admitted. 'I know very little of the ways of the galaxy, or what is expected of me here.'

'I'll be happy to show you around,' Pincushion said. 'My planet has been sending students here for, well, not a long time, but several centuries. We even have a couple of instructors here, at the lower levels.' There was a note of pride in the rendition. 'Maybe one of these millenia we'll manage to place a supervisor.'

Already Dillingham could imagine the prestige that would carry.

At that moment the elevator disgorged another passenger. This was a tall oak-like creature with small leaf-like tentacles fluttering at its side. The bright applicant-band circled the centre bark. It looked at the decorative vines of the apartment and spoke with the whistle of wind through dead branches: 'Appalling captivity.'

The sound of the translations seemed to bring its attention to the other occupants. 'May your probability of acceptance be better than mine,' it said by way of greeting. 'I am a humble modest branch from Treetrunk (the translator learned the naming convention quickly) and despite my formidable knowledge of prosthodontica my percentage is a mere sixty.'

Somewhere in there had been a honk, so Dillingham knew that simultaneous translations were being performed. This device made the little dual-track transcoders seem primitive.

'You are more fortunate than I,' Pincushion replied. 'I stand at only forty-eight per cent.'

They both looked at Dillingham. Pincushion had knobby stalks that were probably eyes, and Treetrunk's apical discs vibrated like the greenery of a poplar sapling.

'Twenty-one per cent,' Dillingham said sheepishly.

There was an awkward silence. 'Well these are only estimates based upon the past performances of your species,' Pincushion said. 'Perhaps your predecessors were not apt.'

'I don't think I *have* any predecessors,' Dillingham said. 'Earth isn't accredited yet.' He hesitated to admit that Earth hadn't even achieved true space travel, by galactic definition.

He had never been embarrassed for his planet before! But he had never had occasion to consider himself a planetary representative before, either.

'Experience and competence count more than some machine's guess, I'm sure,' Treetrunk said. 'I've been practising on my world for six years. If you're—'

'Well, I did practice for ten years on Earth.'

'You see – that will triple your probability when they find out,' Pincushion said encouragingly. 'They just gave you a low probability because no one from your planet has applied before.'

He hoped they were right, but his stomach didn't settle. He doubted that as sophisticated a set-up as the Galactic University would have to stoop to such crude approximation. The administration already knew quite a bit about him from the preliminary application, and his ignorance of galactic method was sure to count heavily against him. 'Are there – references here?' he inquired. 'Facilities? If I could look them over—'

'Good idea!' Pincushion said. 'Come – the operatory is this way, and there is a small museum of equipment.'

There was. The apartment had an annex equipped with an astonishing array of dental technology. There was enough for him to study for years before he could be certain of mastery. He decided to concentrate on the racked texts first, after learning that they could be fed into the translator for ready assimilation in animated projection.

'Standard stuff,' Treetrunk said, making a noise like chafing bark. 'I believe I'll take an estimation.'

As Dillingham returned to the main room with an armful of the box-like texts, the elevator loosed another creature. This was a four-legged cylinder with a head tapered like that of an anteater, and peculiarly thin jointed arms terminating in a series of thorns.

It seemed to him that such physical structure would be virtually ideal for dentistry. The thorns were probably animate rotary burrs, and the elongated snout might reach directly into the patient's mouth for inspection of close work without the imposition of a mirror. After the initial introductions he asked Anteater how his probability stood.

'Ninety-eight per cent,' the creature replied in an offhand manner. 'Our kind seldom miss. We're specialized for this sort of thing.'

Specialization – there was the liability of the human form, Dillingham thought. Men were among the most generalized of Earth's denizens, except for their developed brains – and obviously these galactics had equivalent intellectual potential, and had been in space so long they had been able to adapt physically for something as narrow as dentistry. The outlook for him remained bleak, competitively.

A robot-like individual and a native from Electrolus completed the apartment's complement. Dillingham hadn't known that his sponsor-planet was entering one of its own in the same curriculum, though this didn't affect him particularly.

Six diverse creatures, counting himself – all dentists on their home worlds, all specializing in prosthodontics, all eager to pass the entrance examinations. All male, within reasonable definition – the university was very strict about the proprieties. This was only one apartment in a small city reserved for applicants. The university proper covered the rest of the planet.

They learned all about it that evening at the indoctrination briefing, guided to the lecture-hall by a blue glow manifested on each identification band. The hall was monstrous; only the oxygen-breathers attended this session, but they numbered almost fifty thousand. Other halls catered to differing life-forms simultaneously.

The university graduated over a million highly skilled dentists every term, and had a constant enrollment of twenty million. Dillingham didn't know how many terms it took to graduate – the programmes might be variable – but the incidence of depletion seemed high. Even the total figure represented a very minor proportion of the dentistry in the galaxy. This fraction was extremely important, however, since mere admission as a freshman student here was equivalent to graduation elsewhere.

There were generally only a handful of DU graduates on any civilized planet. These were automatically granted life tenures as instructors at the foremost planetary colleges, or established as consultants for the most challenging cases available. Even the drop-outs had healthy futures.

Instructors for the U itself were drawn from its own most gifted graduates. The top one hundred, approximately – of each class of a million – were siphoned off for special training and retained, and a great number were recruited from the lower ranking body of graduates: individuals who demonstrated superior qualifications in subsequent galactic practice. A few instructors were even recruited from non-graduates, when their specialities were so restricted and their skills so great that such exceptions seemed warranted.

The administrators came largely from the University of Administration, dental division, situated on another planet, and they wielded enormous power. The University President was the virtual dictator of the planet, and his pronouncements had the force of law in dental matters throughout the galaxy. Indeed, Dillingham thought as he absorbed the information, if there were any organization that approached galactic overlordship, it would be the Association of University Presidents. AUP had the authority and the power to quarantine any world found guilty of wilful malpractice in any of the established fields, and since any quarantine covered *all* fields, it was devastating. An abstract was run showing the consequence of the last absolute quarantine: within a year that world had collapsed in anarchy. What followed that was not at all pretty.

Dillingham saw that the level of skill engendered by University training did indeed transcend any ordinary practice. No one on Earth had any inkling of the techniques considered commonplace here. His imagination was saturated with the marvel of it all. His dream of knowledge for the sake of knowledge was a futile one; such training was far too valuable to be reserved for the satisfaction of the individual. No wonder graduates became public servants! The investment was far less monetary than cultural and technological, for the sponsoring planet.

His room-mates were largely unimpressed. 'Everyone knows the universities wield galactic power,' Treetrunk said. 'This is only one school of many, and hardly the most important. Take Finance U, now—'

'Or Transportation U,' Pincushion added. 'Every space ship, every stellar conveyor, designed and operated by graduates of—'

'Or Communication,' Anteater said. 'Comm U has several campuses, even, and they're not dinky little planets like this one, either. Civilization is impossible without communications. What's a few bad teeth, compared to that?'

Dillingham was shocked. 'But all of you are dentists. How can you take such tremendous knowledge and responsibility so casually?'

'Oh, come now,' Anteater said. 'The technology of dentistry hasn't changed in millennia. It's a staid, dated institution. Why get excited?'

'No point in letting ideology go to our heads,' Treetrunk agreed. 'I'm here because this training will set me up for life back home. I won't have to set up a practice at all;

93

I'll be a consultant. It's the best training in the galaxy – we all know that – but we must try to keep it in perspective.'

The others signified agreement. Dillingham saw that he was a minority of one. All the others were interested in the education not for its own sake but for the monetary and prestigious benefits they could derive from a degree.

And all of them had much higher probabilities of admission than he. Was he wrong?

Next day they faced a battery of field tests. Dillingham had to use the operatory equipment to perform specified tasks : excavation, polishing, placement of amalgam, measurement, manufacture of assorted impressions – on a number of familiar and unfamiliar jaws. He had to diagnose and prescribe. He had to demonstrate facility in all phases of laboratory work – facility he now felt woefully deficient in. The equipment was versatile, and he had no particular difficulty adjusting to it, but it was so well made and precise that he was certain his own abilities fell far short of those for whom it was intended.

The early exercises were routine, and he was able to do them easily in the time recommended. Gradually, however, they became more difficult, and he had to concentrate as never before to accomplish the assignments at all, let alone on schedule. There were several jaws so alien that he could not determine their modes of action, and had to pass them by even though the treatment seemed simple enough. This was because he remembered his recent experiences with galactic dentition, and the unsuspected mechanisms of seemingly ordinary teeth, and so refused to perform repairs even on a dummy jaw that might be more harmful than no repair at all.

During the rest breaks he chatted with his companions, all in neighbouring operatories, and learned to his dismay that none of them were having difficulties. 'How can you be sure of the proper occlusal on #17?' he asked Treetrunk. 'There was no upper mandible present for comparison.'

'That was an Oopoo jaw,' Treetrunk rustled negligently. 'Oopoos have no uppers. There's just a bony plate, perfectly regular. Didn't you know that?'

'You recognize all the types of jaw in the galaxy?' Dillingham asked, half jokingly.

'Certainly. I have read at least one text on the dentures of every accredited species. We Treetrunks never forget.'

Eidetic memory! How could a mere man compete with a creature who was able to peruse a million or more texts, and retain every detail of each? He understood more plainly why his probability of admittance was so low. Perhaps even that figure was unrealistically high!

'What was #36, the last one?' Pincushion inquired. 'I didn't recognize it, and I thought I knew them all.'

Treetrunk wilted slightly. 'I never saw that one before,' he admitted. 'It must have been extragalactic, or a theoretic simulacrum designed to test our extrapolation.'

'The work was obvious, however,' Anteater observed. 'I polished it off in four seconds.'

'Four seconds!' All the other were amazed.

'Well, we *are* adapted for this sort of routine,' Anteater said patronizingly. 'Our burrs are built in, and all the rest of it. My main delay is generally in diagnosis. But #36 was a straightforward labial cavity requiring a plastoid substructure and metallic overlay, heated to 540 degrees Centigrade for thirty-seven microseconds.'

'Thirty-nine microseconds,' Treetrunk corrected him, a shade smugly. 'You forgot to allow for the red-shift in the overhead beam. But that's still remarkable time.'

'I employed my natural illumination, naturally,' Anteater said, just as smugly. He flashed a yellow light from his snout.

'No distortion there. But I believe my alloy differs slightly from what is considered standard, which may account for the discrepancy. Your point is well taken, nevertheless. I trust none of the others forgot that adjustment?'

The Electrolyte settled an inch. 'I did,' he confessed.

Dillingham was too stunned to be despondent. Had all of them diagnosed #36 so readily, and were they all so perceptive as to be automatically aware of the wavelength of a particular beam of light? Or were such readings available through the equipment, that he didn't know about, and wouldn't be competent to use if he *did* know? He had pondered that jaw for the full time allotted and finally given it up untouched. True, the cavity had appeared to be perfectly straightforward, but it was too clean to ring true. Could—

The buzzer sounded for the final session and they dispersed to their several compartments.

Dillingham was contemplating #41 with mounting frustration when he heard Treetrunk, via the translator extension, call to Anteater. 'I can't seem to get this S-curve excavation right,' he complained. 'Would you lend me your snout?'

A joke, of course, Dillingham thought. Discussion of cases after they were finished was one thing, but consultation during the exam itself—!

'Certainly,' Anteater replied. He trotted past Dillingham's unit and entered Treetrunk's operatory. There was the muted beep of his high-speed proboscis drill. 'You people confined to manufactured tools labour under such a dreadful disadvantage,' he remarked. 'It's a wonder you can qualify at all !'

'Hmph,' Treetrunk replied good-naturedly . . . and later returned the favour by providing a spot diagnosis based on his memory of an obscure chapter of an ancient text, to settle a case that had Anteater in doubt. 'It isn't as though we're competing against each other,' he said. 'Every point counts !'

Dillingham ploughed away, upset. Of course there had

been nothing in the posted regulations specifically forbidding such procedure, but he had taken it as implied. Even if galactic ethics differed from his own in this respect, he couldn't see his way clear to draw on any knowledge or skill other than his own. Not in this situation.

Meanwhile, #41 was a different kind of problem. The directive, instead of saying 'Do what is necessary', as it had for the #36 they had discussed during the break, was specific. 'Create an appropriate mesiocclusodistal metal-alloy inlay for the afflicted fifth molar in this humanoid jaw.'

This was perfectly feasible. Despite its oddities as judged by Earthly standards, it *was* humanoid and therefore roughly familiar to him. Men did not have more than three molars in a row, but other species did. He had by this time mastered the sophisticated equipment well enough to do the job in a fraction of the time he had required on Earth. He could have the inlay shaped and cast within the time limit.

The trouble was, his experience and observation indicated that the specified reconstruction was not proper in this case. It would require the removal of far more healthy dentin than was necessary, for one thing. In addition, there was evidence of persistent inflammation in the gingival tissue that could herald periodontal disease.

He finally disobeyed the instructions and placed a temporary filling. He hoped he would be given the opportunity to explain his action, though he was afraid he had already failed the exam. There was just too much to do, he knew too little, and the competition was too strong.

The field examination finished in the afternoon, and nothing was scheduled for that evening. Next day the written exam – actually a combination of written, verbal and demonstrative questions – was due, and everyone except Treetrunk was deep in the review texts. Treetrunk was dictating a letter

97

home, his parameter of the translator blanked out so that his narration would not disturb the others.

Dillingham pored over the three-dimensional pictures and captions produced by the tomes while listening to the accompanying lecture. There was so much to master in such a short time! It was fascinating, but he could handle only a tiny fraction of it. He wondered what phenomenal material remained to be presented in the courses themselves, since all the knowledge of the galaxy seemed to be required just to pass the entrance exam. Tooth transplantation? Tissue regeneration? Restoration of living enamel, rather than crude metal fillings?

The elevator opened. A creature rather like a walking oyster emerged. Its yard-wide shell parted to reveal eye-stalks and a comparatively dainty mouth. 'This is the – dental yard?' it inquired timorously.

'Great purple quills!' Pincushion swore quietly. 'One of those insidious panhandlers. I thought they'd cleared such obtusities out long ago.'

Treetrunk, closest to the elevator, looked up and switched on his section of the translator. 'The whole planet is dental, idiot!' he snapped after the query had been repeated for him. 'This is a private dormitory.'

The oyster persisted. 'But you are off-duty dentists? I have a terrible toothache—'

'We are *applicants*,' Treetrunk informed it imperiously. 'What you want is the clinic. Please leave us alone.'

'But the clinic is closed. Please – my jaw pains me so that I can not eat. I am an old clam—'

Treetrunk impatiently switched off the translator and resumed his letter. No one else said anything.

Dillingham could not let this pass. 'Isn't there some regular dentist you can see who can relieve the pain until morning? We are studying for a very important examination.'

'I have no credit – no stiggle – no money for private service,' Oyster wailed. 'The clinic is closed for the night, and my tooth—'

Dillingham looked at the pile of texts before him. He had so little time, and the material was so important. He had to make a good score tomorrow to mitigate today's disaster.

'Please,' Oyster whined. 'It pains me so—'

Dillingham gave up. He was not sure regulations permitted it, but he had to do something. There was a chance he could at least relieve the pain. 'Come with me,' he said.

Pincushion waved his pins, that were actually sensitive celia capable of intricate manoeuvring. 'Not in our operatory,' he protested. 'How can we concentrate with that going on?'

Dillingham restrained his unreasonable anger and took the patient to the elevator. After some errors of navigation he located a vacant testing operatory elsewhere in the application section. Fortunately the translators were everywhere, all keyed to everything, so he could converse with the creature and clarify its complaint.

'The big flat one,' it said as it propped itself awkwardly in the chair and opened its shell. 'It hurts.'

Dillingham took a look. The complaint was valid: most of the teeth had conventional plasticene fillings, but one of these had somehow been dislodged from the proximal surface of a molar: a Class II restoration. The gap was packed with rancid vegetable matter – seaweed? – and was undoubtedly quite uncomfortable for the patient.

'You must understand,' he cautioned the creature, 'that I am not a regular dentist here, or even a student. I have neither the authority nor the competence to do any work of a permanent nature on your teeth. All I can do is clean out the cavity and attempt to relieve the pain so that you can get along until the clinic opens in the morning. Then an authorized dentist can do the job properly. Do you understand?'

'It hurts,' Oyster repeated.

Dillingham located the creature's planet in the directory and punched out the formula for a suitable anaesthetic. The dispenser gurgled and rolled out a cylinder and swab. He squeezed the former and dabbed with the latter around the affected area, hiding his irritation at the patient's evident inability to sit still even for this momentary operation. While waiting for it to take effect, he requested more information from the translator – a versatile instrument.

'Dominant species of Planet Oyster,' the machine reported. 'Highly intelligent, non-specialized, emotionally stable lifeform.' Dillingham tried to reconcile this with what he had already observed of his patient, and concluded that individuals must vary considerably from the norm. He listened to further vital information, and soon had a fair notion of Oyster's general nature and the advisable care of his dentition. There did not seem to be anything to prevent his treating this complaint.

He applied a separator (over the patient's protest) and cleaned out the impacted debris with a spoon excavator without difficulty. But Oyster shied away at the sight of the rotary diamond burr. 'Hurts!' he protested.

'I have given you adequate local anaesthesia,' Dillingham explained. 'You should feel nothing except a slight vibration in your jaw, which will not be uncomfortable. This is a standard drill, the same kind you've seen many times before.' As he spoke he marvelled at what he now termed standard. The burr was shaped like nothing – literally – on Earth, and it rotated at 150,000 r.p.m. – several times the maximum employed back at hime. It was awesomely efficient. 'I must clean the surfaces of the cavity—'

Oyster shut mouth and shell firmly. 'Hurts!' his whisper emerged through clenched defences.

Dillingham thought despairingly of the time this was costing him. If he didn't return to his texts soon, he would forfeit his remaining chance to pass the written exam.

He sighed and put away the power tool. 'Perhaps I can clean it with the hand tools,' he said. 'I'll have to use this rubber dam, though, since this will take more time.'

One look at the patient convinced him otherwise. Regretfully he put aside the rubber square that would have kept the field of operation dry and clean while he worked.

He had to break through the overhanging enamel with a chisel, the patient wincing every time he lifted the mallet and doubling the necessity for the assistant he didn't have. Back on Earth Miss Galland had always calmed the patient. A power mallet would have helped, but that, too, was out. This was as nervous a patient as he had ever had.

It was a tedious and difficult task. He had to scrape off every portion of the ballroom cavity from an awkward angle, hardly able to see what he was doing since he needed a third hand for the dental mirror.

It *would* have to be a Class II – jammed in the side of the molar and facing the adjacent molar, and both teeth so sturdy as to have very little give. A Class II was the very worst restoration to attempt in makeshift fashion. He could have accelerated the process by doing a slipshod job, but it was not in him to skimp even when he knew it was only for a night. Half an hour passed before he performed the toilet: blowing out the loose debris with a jet of warm air, swabbing the interior with alcohol, drying it again.

'Now I'm going to block this up with a temporary wax,' he told Oyster. 'This will not stand up to intensive chewing, but should hold you comfortably until morning.' Not that the warning was likely to make much difference. The trouble had obviously started when the original filling came loose, but it had been weeks since that had happened. Evidently the patient had not bothered to have it fixed until the pain became unbearable – and now that the pain was gone, Oyster might well delay longer, until the work had to be done all over again. The short-sighted refuge from initial inconvenience was hardly a monopoly of Earthly sufferers.

'No,' Oyster said, jolting him back to business. 'Wax tastes bad.'

'This is pseudo-wax – sterile and guaranteed tasteless to most life forms. And it is only for the night. As soon as you report to the clinic—'

'Tastes bad!' the patient insisted, starting to close his shell.

Dillingham wondered again just what the translator had meant by 'highly intelligent . . . emotionally stable'. He kept his peace and dialled for amalgam.

'Nasty colour,' Oyster said.

'But this is pigmented red, to show that the filling is intended as temporary. It will not mar your appearance, in this location. I don't want the clinic to have any misunderstanding.' Or the University administration!

The shell clamped all the way shut, nearly pinning his fingers. 'Nasty colour!', muffled.

More was involved here than capricious difficulty. Did this patient intend to go to the clinic at all? Oyster might be angling for a permanent filling. 'What colour *does* suit you?'

'Gold.' The shell inched open.

It figured. Well, better to humour this patient, rather than try to force him into a more sensible course. Dillingham could make a report to the authorities, who could then roust out Oyster and check the work properly.

At his direction, the panel extruded a ribbon of gold foil.

He placed this in the miniature annealing oven and waited for the slow heat to act.

'You're burning it up!' Oyster protested.

'By no means. It is necessary to make the gold cohesive, for better service. You see—'

'Hot,' Oyster said. So much for helpful explanations. He could have employed noncohesive metal, but this was a lesser technique that did not appeal to him.

At length he had suitable ropes of gold for the slow, delicate task of building up the restoration inside the cavity. The first layer was down; once he malleted it into place—

The elevator burst asunder. A second oyster charged into the operatory waving a translucent tube. 'Villain!' it exclaimed. 'What are you doing to my grandfather?'

Dillingham was taken aback. 'Your *grand*father? I'm trying to make him comfortable until—'

The newcomer would have none of it. 'You're torturing him. My poor, dear, long-suffering grandfather! Monster! How could you?'

'But I'm only—'

Young Oyster levelled the tube at him. Its end was solid, but Dillingham knew it was a genuine weapon. 'Get away from my grandfather. I saw you hammering spikes into his venerable teeth, you sadist! I'm taking him home!'

Dillingham did not move. He considered this a stance of necessity, not courage. 'Not until I complete this work. I can't let him go out like this, with the excavation exposed.'

'Beast! Pervert! *Humanoid!*' the youngster screamed. 'I'll volatize you!'

Searing light beamed from the solid tube. The metal mallet in Dillingham's hand melted and dripped to the floor.

He leaped for the oyster and grappled for the weapon. The giant shell clamped shut on his hand as they fell to the floor. He struggled to right himself, but discovered that the creature had withdrawn all its appendages and now was nothing more than a two-hundred-pound clam – with Dillingham's left hand firmly pinioned.

'Assaulter of innocents!' the youngster squeaked from within the shell. 'Unprovoked attacker! Get your foul paw out of my ear!'

'Friend, I'll be glad to do that – as soon as you let go,' he gasped. What a situation for a dentist!

'Help! Butchery! Genocide!'

Dillingham finally found his footing and hauled on his arm. The shell tilted and lifted from the floor, but gradually let go of the trapped hand. He quickly sat on the shell to prevent it from opening again and surveyed the damage.

Blood trickled from multiple scratches along the wrist, and his hand smarted strenuously, but there was no serious wound.

'Let my grandson go!' the old oyster screamed now. 'You have no right to muzzle him like that! This is a free planet!'

Dillingham marvelled once more at the translator's original description of the species. These just did not seem to be reasonable creatures. He stood up quickly and took the fallen tube.

'Look, gentlemen – I'm very sorry if I have misunderstood your conventions, but I must insist that the young person leave.'

Young Oyster peeped out of his shell. 'Unwholesome creature! Eater of sea-life! How dare you make demands of us?'

Dillingham pointed the tube at him. He had no idea how to fire it, but hoped the creature could be bluffed. 'Please leave at once. I will release your grandfather as soon as the work is done.'

The youngster focused on the weapon and obeyed, grumbling. Dillingham touched the elevator lock the moment he was gone.

The oldster was back in the chair. Somehow the seat adjustment had changed, so that this was now a basket-like receptacle, obviously more comfortable for this patient. 'You are more of a being than you appear,' Oyster remarked. 'I was never able to handle that juvenile so efficiently.'

Dillingham contemplated the droplets of metal splattered on the floor. That heat-beam had been entirely too close – and deadly. His hands began to shake in delayed reaction. He was not a man of violence, and his own quick action had surprised him. The stress of recent events had certainly got to him, he thought ruefully.

'But he's a good lad, really,' Oyster continued. 'A trifle impetuous – but he inherited that from me. I hope you won't report this little misunderstanding.'

He hadn't thought of that, but of course it was his duty to make a complete report on the mêlée and the reason for it. Valuable equipment might have been damaged, not to mention the risk to his own welfare. 'I'm afraid I must,' he said.

'But they are horribly strict!' the oldster protested. 'They will throw him into a foul salty cesspool! They'll boil him in vinegar every hour! His children will be stigmatized!'

'I can't take the law into my own hands.' But of course he already *had*. 'The court – or whatever it is here – must decide. I must make an accurate report.'

'He was only looking out for his ancestor. That's very important to our culture. He's a good—'

The Oyster paused as Dillingham nodded negatively. His shell quivered, and the soft flesh within turned yellow.

Dillingham was alarmed. 'Sir – are you well?'

The translator spoke on its own initiative. 'The Oyster shows the symptoms of severe emotional shock. His health will be endangered unless immediate relief is available.'

All he needed was a dying galactic on top of everything else ! 'How can I help him?' The shell was gradually sagging closed with an insidious suggestiveness.

'The negative emotional stimulus must be alleviated,' the translator said. 'At his age, such disturbances are—'

Dillingham took one more look at the visibly putrefying creature. 'All right !' he shouted desperately. 'I'll withhold my report !'

The collapse ceased. 'You won't tell anyone?' the oldster inquired from the murky depths. 'No matter what?'

'No one.' Dillingham was not at all happy, but saw no other way out. Better silence than a dead patient.

The night was well advanced when he finished with Oyster and sent him home. He had forfeited his study period and, by the time he was able to relax, his sleep as well. He would have to brave the examination without preparation.

It was every bit as bad as he had anticipated. His mind was dull from lack of sleep and his basic fund of information was meagre indeed on the galactic scale. The questions would have been quite difficult even if he had been fully prepared. There were entire categories he had to skip because they concerned specialized procedures buried in his unread review texts. If only he had had time to prepare !

The other were having trouble too. He could see them humped over their tables, or under them, depending on physiology, scribbling notes as they figured ratios and tolerances and indices of material properties. Even Treetrunk looked hard-pressed. If Treetrunk, with a galactic library of dental information filed in his celluloid brain, could wilt with the effort, how could a poor humanoid from a backward planet hope to succeed?

But he carried on to the discouraging end, knowing that his score would damn him but determined to do his best whatever the situation. It seemed increasingly ridiculous, but he still wanted to be admitted to the university. The thought of deserting this stupendous reservoir of information and technique was appalling.

During the afternoon break he collapsed on his bunk and slept. One day remained, one final trial: the interrogation by the Admissions Advisory Council. This, he understood, was the roughest gauntlet of all; more applicants were rejected on the basis of this interview than from both other tests combined.

An outcry woke him in the evening. 'The probabilities are being posted!' Pincushion honked, prodding him with a spine that was not, despite its appearance, sharp.

'Mine's twenty-one per cent, not a penny more,' Dillingham muttered sleepily. 'Low – too low.'

'The *revised* probs!' Pincushion said. 'Based on the test scores. The warning buzzer just sounded.'

Dillingham snapped alert. He remembered now: no results were posted for the field and written exams. Instead the original estimates of acceptance were modified in the light of individual data. This provided unlikely applicants with an opportunity to bow out before submitting themselves to the indignity of a negative recommendation by the AA Council. It also undoubtedly simplified the work of that body by cutting down on the number of interviewees.

They clustered in a tense semi-circle around the main translator. The results would be given in descending order. Dillingham wondered why more privacy in such matters wasn't provided, but assumed that the University had its reasons. Possibly the constant comparisons encouraged better effort, or weeded out the quitters that much sooner.

'Anteater,' the speaker said. It paused. 'Ninety-six per cent.'

Anteater twitched his nose in relief. 'I must have guessed

right on those stress formulations,' he said. 'I knew I was in trouble on those computations.'

'Treetrunk – eighty-five per cent.' Treetrunk almost uprooted himself with glee. 'A twenty-five per cent increase! I must have maxed the written portion after all!'

'Robot – sixty-five per cent.' The robotoid took the news impassively.

The remaining three fidgeted, knowing that their scores had to be lower.

'Pincushion – fifty per cent.' The creature congratulated himself on an even chance, though he had obviously hoped to do better.

'Electrolyte – twenty-three per cent.' The rocklike individual rolled towards his compartment. 'I was afraid of that. I'm going home.'

The rest watched Dillingham sympathetically, anticipating the worst. It came. 'Earthman – three per cent,' the speaker said plainly.

The last reasonable hope was gone. The odds were thirty to one against him, and his faith in miracles was small. The others scattered, embarrassed for him, while Dillingham stood rigid.

He had known he was in trouble – but this! To be given, on the basis of thorough testing, practically no chance of admission. . . .

He was forty-one years old. He felt like crying.

The Admissions Advisory Council was alien even by the standard he had learned in the galaxy. There were only three members – but as soon as this occurred to him, he realized that this would be only the fraction of the Council assigned to his case. There were probably hundreds of interviews going on at this moment, as thousands of applicants were processed.

One member was a honeycomb of gelatinous tissue suspended on a trellislike framework. The second was a mass of purple sponge. The third was an undulating something confined within a tank: a water-breather, assuming that liquid was water. Assuming that it breathed.

The speaker set in the wall of the tank came to life. This was evidently the spokesman, if any were required. 'We do not interview many with so low a probability of admission as student,' Tank said. 'Why did you persist?'

Why indeed? Well, he had nothing further to lose by forthrightness. 'I still want to enter the University. There is still a chance.'

'Your examination results are hardly conducive,' Tank said, and it was amazing how much scorn could be infused into the tone of the mechanical translation. 'While your field exercises were fair, your written effort was incompetent. You appear to be ignorant of all but the most primitive and limited aspects of prosthodontistry. Why should you wish to undertake training for which your capacity is plainly insufficient?'

'Most of the questions of the second examination struck me as relating to basic information, rather than to individual potential,' Dillingham said woodenly. 'If I had that information already, I would not stand in need of the training I came here to learn.'

'An intriguing attitude. We expect, nevertheless, a certain minimum background. Otherwise our curriculum may be wastefully diluted.'

For this Dillingham had no answer. Obviously the ranking specialists of the galaxy should not be used for elementary instruction. He understood the point – yet something in him would not capitulate. There had to be more to this hearing than an automatic decision on the basis of tests whose results could be distorted by participant co-operation (cheating) on the one hand, and circumstantial denial of study-time on the other. Why *have* an advisory board, if that were all?

'We are concerned with certain aspects of your field work,' the honeycomb creature said. He spoke by vibrating his tissues in the air, but the voice emerged from his translator. 'Why did you neglect particular items?'

'Do you mean number seventeen? I was unfamiliar with the specimen and therefore could not repair it competently.'

'You refused to work on it merely because it was new to your experience?' Again the towering scorn.

That did make it sound bad. 'No. I would have done something if I had had more evidence of its nature. But the specimen was not complete. I felt that there was insufficient information presented to justify attempted repairs.'

'You could not have hurt an inert model very much. Surely you realized that even an incorrect repair would have brought you a better score than total failure?'

Dillingham had not known that. 'I assumed that these specimens stood in lieu of actual patients. I gave them the same consideration I would have given a living, feeling creature. Neglect of a cavity in the tooth of a live patient might lead to the eventual loss of that tooth – but an incorrect repair could have caused more serious damage. Sometimes it is better not to interfere.'

'Explain.'

'When I visited the planet Electrolus I saw that the metallic restorations in native teeth were indirectly interfering with communication, which effect was disastrous to the well-being of the individual. This impressed upon me how dangerous well-meaning ignorance could be, even in so simple a matter as a filling.'

'The chairman of the Dental League of planet Electrolus is a University graduate. Are you accusing him of ignorance?'

Oh-oh. 'Perhaps the problem had not come to his attention,' Dillingham said, trying to evade the trap.

'We will return to that matter at another time,' the purple sponge said grimly. Dillingham's reasoning hardly seemed to have impressed this group.

'You likewise ignored item number thirty-six,' Honeycomb said. 'Was your logic the same?'

'Yes. The jaw was so alien to my experience that I could not safely assume that there was anything wrong with it, let alone attempt to fix it. I suppose I was foolish not to fill the labial cavity, in view of your scoring system, but that would have required an assumption I was not equipped to make.'

'How much time did you spend – deciding not to touch the cavity?' Honeycomb inquired sweetly.

'Half an hour.' Pointless to explain that he had gone over every surface of #36 looking for some confirmation that its action was similar to that of any of the jaws with which he was familiar. 'If I may inquire now – what *was* the correct treatment?'

'None. It was a healthy jaw.'

Dillingham's breath caught. 'You mean if I had filled that cavity – what looked like a cavity, I mean—'

'You would have destroyed our model extragalactic patient's health.'

'Then my decision on #36 helped my examination score!'

'No. Your decision was based on uncertainty, not on accurate diagnosis. It threw your application into serious question.'

Dillingham shut his mouth and waited for the next thrust.

'You did not follow instructions on #41,' Honeycomb said. 'Why?'

'I felt the instructions were mistaken. The placement of an MOD inlay was unnecessary for the correction of the condition, and foolish in the face of the peril the tooth was

111

already in from gingivitis. Why perform expensive and complicated reconstruction, when untreated gum disease threatens to nullify it soon anyway?'

'Would that inlay have damaged the function of the tooth in any way?'

'Yes, in the sense that no reconstruction can be expected to perform as well as the original. But even if there were no difference, that placement was functionally unnecessary. The expense and discomfort to the patient must also be considered. The dentist owes it to his patient to advise him of—'

'You are repetitive. Do you place your judgment before that of the University?'

Trouble again. 'I must act on my own best judgment, when I am charged with the responsibility. Perhaps, with University training, I would have been able to make a more informed decision.'

'Kindly delete the pleading,' Honeycomb said.

Something was certainly wrong somewhere. All his conjectures seemed to go against the intent of this institution. Did its standards, as well as its knowledge, differ so radically from his own? Could all his professional and ethical instincts be wrong?

'Your performance on the written examination was extremely poor,' Sponge said. 'Are you naturally stupid, or did you fail to apply yourself properly?'

'I could have done better if I had studied more.'

'You failed to prepare yourself?'

Worse and worse. 'Yes.'

'You were aware of the importance of the examination?'
'Yes.'

'You had suitable review texts on hand?'
'Yes.'

'Yet you did not bother to study them.'

'I wanted to, but—' Then he remembered his promise to

112

the oyster. He could not give his reason for failing to study. If this trio picked up any hint of that episode, it would not relent until everything was exposed. After suffering this much interrogation, he retained no illusions about the likely fate of young Oyster. No wonder the grandfather had been anxious!

'What is your pretext for such neglect?'

'I can offer none.'

The colour of the sponge darkened. 'We are compelled to view with disfavour an applicant who neither applies himself nor cares to excuse his negligence. This is not the behaviour we expect in our students.'

Dillingham said nothing. His position was hopeless – but he still could not give up until they made his rejection final.

Tank resumed the dialogue. 'You have an interesting record. It is even alarming in some respects. You came originally from planet Earth – one of the aborigine cultures. Why did you desert your tribe?'

They had unfortunate ways of putting things! 'I was contacted by a galactic voyager who required prosthodontic repair. I presumed he picked my name out of the local directory.' He described his initial experience with the creatures he had dubbed, facetiously, the North Nebulites, or Enens. Some of that early humour haunted him now.

'You operated on a totally unfamiliar jaw?' Tank demanded abruptly.

'Yes.' Under duress, however. Should he remind them?

'Yet you refused to do similar work on a dummy jaw at this University,' Honeycomb put in.

They were sharp! 'I did what seemed necessary at the time.'

'Don't your standards appear inconsistent, even to you?' Sponge inquired.

Dillingham laughed, not happily. 'Sometimes they do.' How much deeper could he bury his chances?

Tank's turn : 'Why did you accompany the aliens to their world?'

'I did not have much choice, as I explained.'

'So you did not come to space in search of superior prosthodontic techniques?'

'No. It is possible that I might have done so, however, had I known of their availability at the time.'

'Yes, you have repeatedly expressed your recent interest,' Tank said dryly. 'Yet you did not bother to study from the most authoritative texts available on the subject, when you had both opportunity and encouragement to do so.'

Once again his promise to Oyster prevented him from replying. He was coming to understand why his room-mates had shown so little desire to spend time helping the supplicant. Such a gesture appeared, in retrospect, to be a sure passport to failure.

Could he have passed – that is, brought his probability up to a reasonable level – had he turned away that plea? Should he have sacrificed that one creature, for the sake of the hundreds or the thousands he might have helped later, with proper training? He *had* been shortsighted.

But he knew he would do the same thing again, in similar circumstances. He just didn't have the heart to be that practical. At the same time, he could see why the business-like University would have little use for such sentimentality.

'On planet Gleep,' Tank said, surprising him by using his own ludicrous term for the next world he had visited – though of course that was the way the translator had to work – 'you filled a single cavity with twenty-four tons of fine gold alloy.'

'Yes.'

'Are you aware that gold, however plentiful it may be

on Gleep, remains an exceptionally valuable commodity in the galaxy? Why did you not develop a less extravagant substitute?'

Dillingham tried to explain about the awkwardness of the situation, about the pressure of working within the cavernous mouth of a three-hundred foot sea creature, but it did seem that he had made a mistake. He could have employed a specialized cobalt-chromium-molybdenum alloy that would have been strong, hard, resilient and resistive to corrosion, and that might well have been superior to gold in that particular case. He had worried, for example, about the weight of such a mass of gold, and this alternate, far lighter material, would have alleviated that concern. It was also much cheaper stuff. He had not thought carefully enough about such things at the time. He said so.

'Didn't you consult your Enen associates?'

'I couldn't. The English/Enen transcoder was broken.' But that was no excuse for not having had them develop the chrome-cobalt alloy earlier. He had allowed his personal preference for the more familiar gold to halt his quest for improvement.

'Yet you *did* communicate with them later, surmounting that problem readily once the gold had been wasted.'

Dillingham was becoming uncomfortably aware that this group had done its homework. The members seemed to know everything about him. 'I discovered by accident that the English/Gleep and Gleep/Enen transcoders could be used in concert. I had not realized that at the time we were casting the filling.'

'Because you were preoccupied with the immediate problem?'

'I think so.'

'But not too preoccupied to notice decay in the neighbouring teeth.'

'No.' It did seem foolish now, to have been so concerned with future dental problems, while wasting tons of valuable metal on the work in progress. How did that jibe with his more recent concern for Oyster's problem, to the exclusion of the much larger University picture? Was there any coherent rationale to his actions, or was he continually rationalizing to excuse his errors of judgment?

Was the seeming unfairness of this interview merely a way of proving this to him?

But Tank wasn't finished. 'You next embarked with a passing diplomat of uncertain reputation who suggested a way to free you from your commitment to Gleep.'

'He was very kind.' Dillingham did not regret his association with Trach, the friendly dinosaur.

'He resembled one of the vicious predators of your planet's past – yet you trusted your person aboard his ship?'

'I felt, in the face of galactic diversity of species, that it was foolish to judge by appearances. One has to be prepared to extend trust, if one wants to receive it.'

'You believe that?' Honeycomb demanded instantly.

'I try to.' It was so hard to defend himself against the concentrated suspicion of the council.

'You do not seem to trust the common directives of this University, however.'

What answer could he make to that? They had him in another conflict, since they chose to interpret it that way.

'Whereupon you proceeded to investigate *another* unfamiliar jaw,' Tank said. 'Contrary to your expressed policy. Why?'

'Trach had befriended me, and I wanted to help him.'

'So you put friendship above policy,' Sponge said. 'Convenient.'

'And did you help him?' Tank again. It was hard to remember who said what, since they were all so murderously sharp.

'Yes. I adapted a sonic instrument that enabled him to clean his teeth efficiently.'

'And what was your professional fee for this service?'

Dillingham reined his mounting temper. 'Nothing. I was not thinking in such terms.'

'A moment ago you were quite concerned about costs.'

'I was concerned about unnecessary expense to the patient. That strikes me as another matter.'

'And of course the prospective sale of your contract to planet Ra had no bearing on your decision to help a friend,' Honeycomb said with infinite irony.

Sponge spoke before Dillingham could respond. 'And the dinosaur told you about the University of Dentistry?'

'Yes, among other things. We conversed quite a bit.'

'And so you decided to attend, on hearsay evidence.'

'That's not fair!'

'Is the colour of your face a sign of distress?'

He realized that they were deliberately needling him, so he shut up. Why should he allow himself to get excited over a minor slur, after passing over major ones? All he could do that way was prove he was unstable, and therefore unfit.

'And did you seriously believe,' Sponge persisted nastily, 'that you had any chance at all to be admitted as a student here?'

Again he had no answer.

'On planet Electrolus you provoked a war by careless advice,' Honeycomb said. 'Whereupon you conspired to be exiled – to this University. What kind of reception did you anticipate here, after such machinations?'

So that was it! What use to explain that he had *not* schemed, that Trach had cleverly found a solution to the

Electrolus political problem that satisfied all parties? This trio would only twist that into further condemnation.

'I made mistakes on that planet, as I did elsewhere,' he said at last. 'I hoped to learn to avoid such errors in the future by enrolling in a corrective course of instruction. It was ignorance, not devious intent, that betrayed me. I still think this University has much to offer me.'

'The question before us,' Tank said portentously, 'is what *you* have to offer the University. Have you any further statements you fancy might influence our decision?'

'I gather from your choice of expression that it has already been made. In that case I won't waste any more of your time. I am ready for it.'

'We find you unsuitable for enrollment at this University as a student,' Tank said. 'Please depart by the opposite door.'

So as not to obstruct the incoming interviewees. Very neat. Dillingham stood up wearily. 'Thank you for your consideration,' he said formally, keeping the irony out of his tone. He walked to the indicated exit.

'One moment, ex-applicant,' Honeycomb said. 'What are your present plans?'

Dillingham wondered why the creature bothered to ask. 'I suppose I'll return to practice wherever I'm needed – or wanted,' he said. 'I may not be the finest dentist available, or even adequate by your standards – but I love my profession, and there is much I can still do.' But why was it that the thought of returning to Earth, that he was free to do now and where he *was* adequate, no longer appealed? Had the wonders he had glimpsed here spoiled him for the backwoods existence? 'I would have preferred to add the University training to my experience, but there is no reason to give up what I already have just because my dream has been denied.'

He walked away from them.

The hall did not lead to the familiar elevators. Instead, absent-mindedly following the wrist-band glow, he found himself in an elegant apartment. He turned, embarrassed to have blundered into the wrong area, but a voice stopped him.

'Please be seated, Earthman.'

It was the old Oyster he had treated two days before. Dillingham was not adept at telling aliens of identical species apart, but he could not mistake this one. 'What are you doing here?'

'We all have to dwell somewhere.' Oyster indicated a couch adaptable to a wide variety of forms. 'Make yourself comfortable. I have thoughts to exchange with you.'

Dillingham marvelled at the change in the manner of his erstwhile patient. This was no longer a suffering, unreasonable indigent. But his presence remained incongruous.

'Surely it occurred to you, Doctor, that there are only three groups upon this planet? The applicants, the students – and the University personnel. Which of these do you suppose should lack proper dental care? Which should lack the typical University identification?'

'You—' Dillingham stared at him, suddenly making connections. 'You have no band – but the elevator worked for you! You're an employee! It was a put-up job!'

'It was part of your examination.'

'I failed.'

'What gave you that impression?'

Brother! 'The Admissions Advisory Council found me unfit to enter this University.'

'I find that hard to believe, Doctor.'

Dillingham faced him angrily, not appreciating this business at all. 'I don't know why you or the University were so eager to interfere with my application, but you succeeded nicely. They rejected me.'

'Perhaps we should verify this,' Oyster said, unperturbed.

He spoke into the translator: 'Summon Dr. Dillingham's advisory group.'

They came: the Sponge, the Honeycomb and the Tank, riding low conveyors. 'Sir,' they said respectfully.

'What was your decision with regard to this man's application?'

Tank replied. 'We found this humanoid to be unsuitable for enrollment at this University as a student.'

Dillingham nodded. Whatever internecine politics were going on here, at least that point was clear.

'Did you discover this applicant to be deficient in integrity?' Oyster inquired softly. It was the gentle tone of complete authority.

'No sir,' Tank said.

'Professional ethics?'

'No sir.'

'Professional caution?'

'No sir.'

'Humility?'

'No sir.'

'Temper control?'

'No sir.'

'Compassion? Courage? Equilibrium?'

'That is for you to say, sir.'

Oyster glanced at Dillingham. 'So it would seem. What, then, gentlemen, *did* you find the applicant suitable for?'

'Administration, sir.'

'Indeed. Dismissed, gentlemen.'

'Yes, Director.' The three departed hastily.

Dillingham started. 'Yes, *who*?'

'There is, you see, a qualitative distinction between the potential manual trainee and the potential administrator,' Oyster said. 'Your room-mates were evaluated as students – and they certainly have things to learn. Oh, technically they are proficient enough – quite skilled, in fact, though none had the opportunity to exhibit the depth of competence manifested in adversity that you did. But in attitude – well, there will be considerable improvement there, or they will hardly graduate from *this* school. I daresay you know what I mean.'

So the cheating had been noted ! 'But—'

'We are equipped to inculcate manual dexterity and technical comprehension. Of course the techniques tested in the Admissions Examination are primitive; none are employed in advanced restoration. Our interrogatory schedule is principally advisory, to enable us to programme for individual needs.

'Character, on the other hand, is far more difficult to train – or to assess accurately in a fixed situation. It is far more reliable if it comes naturally, which is one reason we don't always draw from graduates, or even promising students. We are quite quick to investigate applicants possessing the personality traits we require, and this had nothing to do with planet or species. A promising candidate may emerge from any culture, even the most backward, and is guaranteed from none. No statistical survey is reliable in pinpointing the individual we want. In exceptional cases it becomes a personal matter, a non-objective thing. Do you follow me?'

Dillingham's mind was whirling. 'It sounds almost as though you want me to—'

'To undertake training at University expense leading to the eventual assumption of my own position : Director of the School of Prosthodontics.'

Dillingham was speechless.

'I am anticipating a promotion, you see,' Oyster confided. 'The vacancy I leave is my responsibility. I would not suffer a successor to whom I would not trust the care of my own teeth.'

'But I couldn't possibly – I haven't the—'

'Have no concern. You adapted beautifully when thrust from your protected environment into galactic society, and this will be no more difficult. The University of Administration has a comprehensive programme that will guarantee your competence for the position, and of course you will serve as my assistant for several years until you get the hang of it. We are not rushed. You will not be subjected to the ordeal unprepared; that unpleasantness is over.'

Dillingham still found this hard to grasp. 'Your grandson – what if I'd—'

'I shall have to introduce you more formally to that young security officer. He is not, unfortunately, my grandson; but he is the finest shot with the single-charge laser on the planet. We try to make our little skits realistic.'

Dillingham remembered the metal mallet dripping to the floor: no freak interception after all. And the way the youngster had retreated before the tube . . . that, being single-shot, was no longer functional. Realism, yes.

That reminded him. 'That tooth of yours I filled. I *know* that wasn't—'

'Wasn't fake. You are correct. I nursed that cavity for three months, using it to check out prospects. It is a very good thing I won't need it any more, because you spoiled it utterly.'

'I—'

'You did such a competent job that I should have to have a new cavity cultured for my purpose. No experienced practitioner would mistake it now for a long-neglected case even if I yanked out the gold and re-impacted the cavity. *That*, Doctor, is the skill that impresses me – the skill that remains after the machinery has been incapacitated. Good intentions mean nothing unless backed by authoritative discretion and ability. You were very slow, but you handled that deliberately obstructive patient very well. Had it been otherwise—'

'But why me? You could have selected anyone—'

Oyster put a friendly smile into his voice. 'Hardly, Doctor. I visited eleven dormitories that evening before I came to yours – with no success. All contained prospects whose record and fieldwork showed that particular potential. You selected yourself from this number and carried it through honourably. More correctly, you presented yourself as a candidate for the office; we took it from there.'

'You certainly did !'

'Portions of your prior record were hard to believe, I admit. It was incredible that a person who had as little galactic background as you did should accomplish so much. But now we are satisfied that you do have the touch, the ability to do the right thing in an awkward or unfamiliar situation. That, too, is essential for the position.'

Dillingham fastened on one incongruity. 'I – I selected *myself*?'

'Yes, Doctor. When you demonstrated your priorities.'

'My priorities? I don't—'

'When you sacrificed invaluable study time to offer assistance to a creature you believed was in pain.'

Her heart sank when she saw Ra. There was no green on the surface of the planet; the entire landscape seemed to consist of tailings from the mines, mounded into mountains and eroded into valleys.

Radium mines – she had realized the significance of that too late. They were notorious throughout the galaxy for the effect they had on living creatures. The local ore, called pitchcar, was extraordinarily rich; thus it required only fifty tons of the stuff to produce a full ounce of radium. The non-commercial byproducts such as uranium were discarded wherever convenient. There was no trash collection here.

If Dr. Dillingham had come to this planet. . . .

The ship landed ungently. The front port burst open, admitting a foul cloud of native smog, and several troll-like tripeds stomped in. One spoke, his voice like dry bones being run through an unoiled grinder.

'Slaves of Ra,' the central translator rasped, the words muffled by the babble of other renditions for the dubious benefit of a score of miserable species. 'Co-operate, and you may survive for years. Malinger, and you will receive inclement assignments. Any questions?'

Judy felt sorry for the prisoners, but knew there was nothing at all she could do for them now.

'Sir,' a lovely ladybug called melodiously. 'We do not wish to seem ungrateful, but we are very hungry—'

True enough. There had been no food aboard, and the trip had lasted sixteen hours. Many galactic species had much more active metabolisms than human beings did, and there was no telling how long they had been hungry before she embarked.

'The others will be hauled to the force-feeding station after processing. *You* will wait for the following shift for sustenance, with half-rations for the first two days of your inclement assignment. Any other questions?'

There were none. The hapless prisoners had got the message.

'Now step out promptly as I call your names. Aardvark!'

A creature vaguely resembling its Earthly namesake emerged from its cramped compartment and shambled forward.

'Too slow!' the translator barked. A troll aimed a rod. A beam of energy stabbed out. A patch of fur on Aardvark's rump burst into flame, and the odour of scorched flesh drifted back. He broke into a gallop.

Judy had not quite believed the pessimism of the prisoners as they travelled, though she had talked with several. She had been naïve. This was horrible!

'Bugbear!'

A beetle the size of a bear lumbered hastily out, as well it might: a touch of the laser would puncture its thin shell and send its juices spewing.

'Cricketleg!' The next jumped down. Judy wondered how the rollcall came to be alphabetical in English, since the translator assigned names purely by convenience of description. This was merely another mystery of galactic technology.

'Dogface!' He yelped as the beam singed his tail.

'Earthgirl!'

Judy froze. It couldn't be! She was only here to—

A troll tramped down the aisle, poking his beamer ahead aggressively. He braced his three knobbly legs, reached out with a hairy arm, and grasped her hair in one hank. He yanked.

'No!' she cried, her eyes pulled round by the tension on her hair. 'I'm only visiting! I'm not a prisoner!'

The troll hauled her up until she stood on tiptoes to ease the pain. '*Visiting!* Hee, hee, hee!' He aimed the beamer at her face.

'Trach!' she screamed. 'Trach of Trachos! I'm here to see him!'

'A malingerer,' the troll said with satisfaction. 'I shall made an example. First I shall vaporize her squat snout.' He flicked one of his four thumbs over a setting on the beamer and pressed the business end against her nose.

'One moment, troll,' the translator said. Such instruments were versatile, serving as telephones and radios as well as language transposers. 'I believe I heard my name.'

The triped hesitated, grimacing. 'Who are you, butting into private entertainment?'

'Trach, naturally. Be so kind as to deliver that creature to me, undamaged.'

'I don't know no Trach!'

'Oh? Here is my identification.' A phonetic blob sounded.

'Hm,' the troll said, disgruntled. 'That Trach. Well, send her on to the branding station when you're through with her.'

Shoved roughly out, Judy pinned up her hurting hair temporarily and followed the translator's instructions to reach Trach's office. 'Turn right, prisoner,' the unit outside the ship snapped. She turned right; the other miserable aliens turned left, headed for the dismal rigours of processing. She felt guilty.

The spaceport, despite its choking atmosphere, was enclosed. She could make out the blowing dust beyond the grimy window panels, showing that it was actually worse outside. She heard the shriek of ore-bearing vehicles and saw a line of bedraggled workers headed for the arid entrance to a mine.

'Up the stairs, malingerer,' the next unit said. She climbed flight after flight of cruelly steep rough stone steps. A panel on a landing gave her a view of a Ra graveyard : bones and clothing and shells and assorted other durable elements of assorted creatures. There was no attempt at burial.

'Third chamber down, weakling.' She found the place and touched the door-signal.

'Enter,' a differently-toned, more pleasant translator said from within. She was tempted to point out that it had forgotten the customary expletive.

She edged the bleak metal door open. The chamber was empty. She heard water running and saw fog near the ceiling. Someone was having a shower !

'I'll be right out,' the pleasantly modulated voice said from the direction of the shower. It sounded real – as though spoken in English rather than translated. Unlikely, of course; she had encountered no one from Earth since answering that fateful ad.

The water noise stopped. Trach whistled cheerily as he

dried himself in the other room. In a moment she heard his feet on the floor as he dressed. He sounded heavy. 'You're Miss Galland of Earth,' he called. 'The muck-a-muck of Gleep notified me.'

'You're not using a translator!' she exclaimed.

'I never bother,' he admitted, still out of her sight. 'Now where is my jacket? Can't entertain a lady undressed, ha-ha.'

'Dr. Dillingham – is he here?'

'I'm afraid not. He left Electrolus for the University. He's undertaking administrative training now. I'm sorry to inform you that you made your trip here for nothing.' His solid footsteps approached.

'Oh, no, I'm *glad* he's not here ! I mean—'

Then she saw Trach. A literal, twelve-foot dinosaur.

'My dear, you look good enough to eat,' he said, smiling. He had two thousand teeth.

She was not the fainting type. She fainted.

CHAPTER SIX

'An administrator,' Oyster said, 'has to be prepared to tackle problems that are beyond the capabilities of his subordinates.'

'Of course,' Dr. Dillingham agreed, but he didn't quite like the way the bivalved director said it. This was his first day back from his initial quartermester at the University of Administration, and though his Certificate of Potential Administration was in good order he hardly felt qualified for the job he faced. Of course this was only an interim experience-term, after which he would return for more advanced administrative training – but he had a nasty suspicion that Oyster wasn't going to let him off lightly.

'We've had a call from Metallica, one of the Robotoid planets,' the Director said. Dillingham wondered what the real terms were for planets and species, but of course he would never know. Probably 'man' was rendered in the other galactic languages as 'hairy grub' . . . 'The natives have an awkward situation, and our field representative bounced it on up to us. I'm not sure it's strictly a prosthodontic matter, but we'd best take a look.'

Dillingham relaxed. For a moment he had been afraid that he was about to be sent out alone. But of course Oyster would have him watch a few missions before trusting him to uphold the University's reputation by diagnosing a field problem himself. Every move a Director made was galactic news. Minor news, to be sure – but a blunder would rapidly rebound.

'I have reserved accommodation for three,' Oyster said briskly. His large shell gave his voice an authoritative reverberation the translator dutifully emulated. 'It will be a forty-eight hour excursion, so have your appointments re-scheduled accordingly.'

'Passage for three?' Dillingham had no appointments yet, as Oyster well knew.

'My secretary will accompany us, naturally. Miss Tarantula.' The translator meant well, but the name gave him a start. 'She's very efficient. Grasps the struggling essence immediately and sucks the blood right out of it, so to speak.'

Just so.

A University limousine carried them past the student picket line and whisked them the three light-minutes to the transport terminal. Dillingham wondered what the students had on their collective mind. He had observed one of their demonstrations on his way in, but had not had the opportunity to inquire further.

Miss Tarantula was there ahead of them with the reservations. Her eight spiked spiderlegs bustled Oyster and Man busily into the elevator entering the galactic liner. She also carried suitcase and equipment.

'Please give Dr. Dillingham a synopsis of the problem,' Oyster said once they were ensconced in their travelling compartment. The ubiquitous translator was built into the wall, and the acoustics were such that the Director seemed to be talking English. 'While I snooze.' With that he pulled in his arms and legs and closed his shell.

'Certainly.' Miss Tarantula was busily stringing threads across her section, fashioning a shimmering web. She did not interrupt this chore as she spoke. 'Metallica is one of the more backward Robotoid worlds, having been devastated some millennia ago in the course of the fabled Jann uprising. Archaeological excavations are currently in progress in an effort to uncover Jann artifacts and reconstruct the mundane elements of their unique civilization. It was thought that all the Jann had been destroyed, but now they have discovered one in the subterranean wreckage.'

'It's skeleton, you mean,' Dillingham interrupted.

'No, Director. A complete robot.'

Oops. He had forgotten that they were dealing with a robotoid culture. Metal and ceramics instead of flesh and bones. 'Must be pretty well rusted or corroded, though.'

'Jann don't corrode. They're super-robots, invulnerable to normal forces and virtually immortal. This one happened to be incapacitated by—'

'You mean it's *alive*? After thousands of years?'

'As alive as a robot ever is, Director.' She had completed her web and was now settled in it for the journey, her body completely suspended. It seemed to be an effective acceleration harness, though a liner of this type required no such precautions. 'But this one can't function because it has a toothache. The natives don't dare approach it, but the excavation can't continue until it is removed. So they notified the University.'

Dillingham whistled inwardly. That must be a phenomenal toothache, to freeze an immortal, invulnerable superrobot for over a thousand years. He was glad Oyster was handling this one; it would be educational to witness.

But what, he wondered, would they do with the Jann after its toothache had been cured? And what did a robot want with *teeth*? The ones he had met, dentists though they might be, had no proper mouths and did not eat.

Metallica *was* backward. Its spaceport resembled a junkyard, with corroding hulks at its fringe. A single dilapidated tower guided the liner in, and there was no landing net to clasp it invisibly in deep space and set it down with gentle precision. Their welcome, however, was warm enough.

'Director!' a small green robot said through a rickety

mobile transcoder it trundled behind. 'We've been sleepless awaiting your gracious arrival.'

Miss Tarantula emitted a hiss reminiscent of a matron's sniff. 'Robots never sleep anyway.'

'We haven't eaten a thing, we were so eager for your Lordship to come.'

'Robots don't eat, either,' she pointed out.

The green robot turned about, lifted one metal foot, and delivered a clanging kick to the pedestal of the transcoder. There was a pained screech and a series of metallic burps. Then: 'We have watched no television in two days.'

'That's more like it,' Miss Tarantula said, permitting herself to be mollified. 'A robot who loses its appetite for television is becoming almost sentient, and that's a sure sign of distress. Better have the spools updated on that contraption before someone has a misunderstanding.'

With a secretary like that, Dillingham realized, an administrator could hardly err. He was glad that the three of them carried University three-language transcoders for private dialogue. There was a subtle distinction in principle between the small transcoders and the large translators; he didn't understand the technical part, but knew that the 'coder differed from the 'lator as a motorcycle differed from a jet plane. But the 'coders were portable and self-contained and cheap, so remained in common use on backward planets. Insert the proper spools and hold an adequate conversation. Usually.

'What seems to be the difficulty?' Oyster inquired in an offshell manner. Dillingham was reminded of one of the dictums of effective administration: Never ask a question of a client without first knowing most of the answer.

The little robot began volubly defining the problem. Dillingham's attention wandered, for Miss Tarantula's summary had been far more succinct. How, he wondered, did robots reproduce? Were there male and female mechanicals, and did they marry? Were there procreative taboos, metal pornography, broken iron hearts?

'Director,' Miss Tarantula said on their private link-up.

Oyster angled his transcoder intake – he wore the device inside his huge shell – unobtrusively at her, not interrupting the green robot's narrative. Dillingham did likewise.

'There is a priority call from the University.' She had a trans-star receiver somewhere on her complicated person. 'A wildcat student demonstration has infiltrated your wing. They're raiding the files—'

Oyster's eye-stalks turned bright green. 'Boiling oceans!' he swore.

The robot broke off. 'Did you say "gritty oil", Director?' The vibration of its headpiece showed it was upset.

'Take over, Director!' Oyster snapped at Dillingham. 'I'm summoning an emergency ship back. My files!' And he ran across the landing field towards the communications station as rapidly as his spindly legs would carry him. Miss Tarantula followed.

'Did he say "gritty oil"?' the green robot demanded insistently. There was a faint odour of burning insulation about it. 'He may be a Very Important Sentient, but language like that—'

'Of course not,' Dillingham said quickly. 'He would never stoop to such uncouthness. It must be a scratch on the transcoder spool.' But he suspected that the transcoder had correctly rendered the expletive. His own unit had not been programmed for gutter talk; otherwise his own ears might be burning. Oyster had certainly been furious.

'Oh,' the robot said, disgruntled. 'Well, as I was saying – er, you *are* going to solve the problem, even if he renigs?'

'Naturally.' Dillingham hoped the quiver in his voice sounded like confidence. 'The Director did not renig; he merely left the matter in my hands. The University always honours its commitments.' But privately he preferred the robot's term. He should have known he'd find himself in over his ears without a facemask. Somehow it always happened that way. 'I suppose I'd better see the patient now.'

Frantically eager – who claimed robots had no emotions! – the official conducted him to the site of the excavations. They rode in an antique floater past high mounds of broken rock. There were plants in this world, but the few he saw had a metallic look. Hardly a place for a human being to reside, though the air was breathable and the temperature and gravity comfortable.

The vehicle stopped, settling to the ground with a flatulent sigh. 'I dare go no further,' the green robot said, and indeed his headpiece was rattling in a fear-feedback. 'The Jann is in the next pit. Signal when you're finished, and I will pick you up again. If it's safe.'

As Dillingham stepped down with his bag of equipment, the robot spun the cart around, goosed the motor, and floated swiftly back the way they had come – taking the transcoder and signal with it.

Stranded again! What kind of robot could it be, that even other robots feared so greatly? And if it were that dangerous, why hadn't they simply destroyed it? Oh – it was reputed to be invulnerable.

He walked to the pit and peered down.

A tremendous robot lay there, half buried in rubble. Judging from the proportion exposed, it had to be twelve feet long entire. Its armour was polished to a glass-like finish despite the centuries of weathering and abrasion. It was an awesome sight, and the mighty torso seemed to pulse with power. A cruel, thin keening smote his ears, and he knew it at once for the robotic note of pain. He had not learned much about robots, but he was sensitive to distress in anything, flesh, metal or other. Yes, this creature was alive – and suffering. That was all he really needed to know.

The head section was roughly cubical and two feet on a side. A drawer in the region that would have been the face of a man was partially out, half-full of sand, and within this something glowed. Robots did not ordinarily have mouths, but some models did have orifices for the intromission and processing of assorted substances. The gears that ground down hard samples could be considered as teeth.

Now that he was in the physical presence of the patient, the information in one of the University cram-courses began to come to the surface. He was, he realized, familiar with the basic procedures for repairing such equipment. But the specific type he found here was particularly awkward, and if he operated on it he risked making some serious mistake. This was a most sophisticated robot, and it had been listed as extinct.

But if its innards followed the principles of contemporary robots, its 'teeth' might serve a double purpose. They would have an extremely hard exterior surface for manual crushing action, together with intricate internal circuitry for communications and processing of data. As with the Electrolytes. That meant that a malfunction in a tooth could distort far more than the mechanical operation of the mouth. A short-circuit could interfere with the functions of the brain itself. . . .

Dillingham vacuumed out the sand and studied the configuration. One tooth glowed hotly. The pain-hum seemed to emanate from it. A quick check with his precise University instruments verified the short-circuit.

'All right, Jann – I believe I have diagnosed the condition,' he said, speaking rhetorically while he set up the necessary paraphernalia. He doubted that the giant robot could hear or comprehend anything in its present state. 'Unfortunately, I am not equipped to operate on the unit itself, and I don't have a replacement. I'll have to relieve the pain by bridging around the tooth – in essence, shorting out the short. This is crude, and will render the tooth inoperative, but unless it is a critical unit the rest of your system should be able to function. You'll have to seek help at a thoroughly equipped robotoid clinic to have that tooth replaced, however, and I wouldn't delay if I were you. My jury-rig won't be any too stable, and you don't want a relapse.'

Yet it would have been simple for a native dentist to bridge the tooth. Why hadn't that been done? What were they so afraid of, to allow an ancient cousin to suffer unnecessarily like this? Surely a single Jann, the only survivor of its kind, could not imperil a planet, even if it should have a mind to. And if it *were* that dangerous, the fact that a University dentist had repaired it would not dispose it any more kindly towards the errant locals.

Too bad he hadn't had a chance to review the history of the Jann uprising. Maybe some of these annoying inconsistencies would have been explained. But with Oyster running off so suddenly . . . well, this creature was in pain and needed help.

He was ready. He applied the bridge and soldered the terminals. The job itself was nothing; the skill had been required for the electronic preparations, the verification of tolerances, the location of circuits. It would have been a mistake to remove the tooth, for it was in series with the others so that the extraction could have been fatal for the patient. And many robots, his cram-course said, were programmed to self-destruct when killed. They were living bombs.

The keening faded. The bypassed tooth began to cool. The Jann moved one glittering arm a few inches. 'Nnnnn,' it said, the sound emerging from a grill in its forehead. A bulb set in the side of its head began to glow softly. An eye?

Relieved but apprehensive now that the job had been done, Dillingham stood back and awaited developments. He wanted to be sure his field surgery had been effective, as a matter of professional pride and compassion. Should the patient seem to be worse, he would have to undo his handiwork and try again.

The earth and rock around the Jann's nether portions cracked and bucked. A sleek massive foot ripped out of the ground, spraying fragments of rock in a semi-circle. The Jann hefted its body, moving its shining limbs with ponderous splendour. It was a magnificent hunk of machinery.

'Nnonne,' it said on hands and knees, raising its head to cover Dillingham with a small antenna.

Was that a groan or a comment? Of course it would speak a strange language, assuming it used vocal communication at all, and his little Oyster/Tarantula/English transcoder would be useless without the appropriate spool. He would have to judge by the robot's actions and manner.

The Jann stood, towering monstrously above him. 'None but I,' it said, the volume deafening, the tones reverberating as though emanating from the lower register of a mighty organ.

None but I? That sounded perilously like English, and it hadn't come through the transcoder.

'Are you – do you—?' Dillingham faltered. Even if this Jann embodied a full translator, it could hardly have a setting for English. It had been buried for tens of centuries!

The Jann peered down at him with prismatic lenses that opened from a formerly blank area of its head. Sunlight glinted from its stainless torso and wisps of steam rose from its fingertips, giving it the aspect of a rainbow in fog. 'NONE BUT I,' it boomed, 'SHALL DO THEE DIE!'

Oh-oh.

'There seems to be a misunderhension,' Dillingham said,

136

backing away as surreptitiously as he could manage. 'I mean misapprestanding . . .' He whistled ineffectively. 'I wasn't – I didn't – I mean, I *fixed* your tooth, or at least—' He tripped over a rock and sat down abruptly.

The Jann stepped towards him, and the earth shuddered. 'Thou didst release me from mine bondage,' it said, moderating its volume but none of its timbre. 'Thou didst bypass the short.'

Dillingham pushed himself back without getting up. 'Yes. Yes! That's the idea.'

The Jann reached forth a scintillating arm and pointed a finger oddly like a cannon at Dillingham's head. 'Listen, mortal, for I have somewhat to impart to thee.'

Dillingham froze where he was. He did not like the giant's attitude – in fact, he was terrified – but there was no point in acting precipitously.

'In the days and years of strife between the tribes of the Jann and the minor ilk,' it said, 'it was my misfortune to bite down carelessly on a button-grenade and so befoul a circuit, nor could I recover the use of my body while that geis was upon me, though my mind was sound except for the pain. And so when I was buried thereafter by refuse my companions located me not, for it was wartime and there was much electrostatic interference and other distraction, and they thought me defunct. I perceived all manner of newsbands and converse in my area, as was my wont, but could not respond, and great was my suffering. In that pit I abode an thousand years, during which I said in my heart, "Whoso shall release me, him will I enrich for ever and ever." But the full millennium went by, and when no one set me free I entered upon the second thousand saying, "Whoso shall release me, for him will I fulfil three wishes." Yet no one set me free. Thereupon I waxed wroth with exceeding wrath and said to myself, "Whoso shall release me from this time forth, no one but I shall do him die." And now, as thou hast released me, needs must I honour that oath.'

It was obvious to Dillingham that he faced a deranged robot. That bypassed tooth must have contained an important sanity circuit. But it was too late to undo the damage; the Jann would hardly let him near that tooth again. It would, in fact, kill him first.

But the story sounded familiar. The Jann, imprisoned – that was it? The spirit in the bottle, sworn to kill whoever released him. A fisherman had brought up the bottle in his net and unwittingly uncorked it. . . .

Dillingham understood, now, why the locals had been so chary of this patient. Who wanted to gamble on the particular oath in force at the moment of release?

How had that fisherman got out of it? There had been a gimmick—

The Jann stumbled, and Dillingham lunged away from it. 'My powerpack is almost depleted!' the robot lamented. 'Four thousand years of that accursed short-circuit, yet I preserved my life-power until this moment! Had it not been my caution-synapse you bridged out, I would have realized the danger before expending power recklessly in breaking out of the rock and defining my motive. I can hardly move!'

Good news! Dillingham scrambled up the side of the pit and ran.

'O mortal!' the great voice called after him. 'Wouldst desert me in this sad state, and my power insufficient to free myself from this ugly hole?'

Dillingham cursed himself for his stupidity, but was oddly moved by the plea. He stopped. 'Will you change your mind about killing me, if I help you again?'

'Mortal, I can not gainsay an oath of twenty centuries. None but I shall do thee die.'

'Then why should I help you?'

But the Jann, having exhausted its small remaining charge, could only repeat in fading resonance, 'None but I . . .'

Against his better judgment, Dillingham returned to the pit and peeked down. The Jann lay sprawled at the bottom, its head-bulb dim.

He sighed with relief and began the long hike back to the spaceport. He had, at any rate, performed his mission. He had cured the toothache. His only concern now was to get back to the University.

He walked for hours. His bag grew heavy, but he refused to discard it. His feet developed blisters and his tongue became parched, but there seemed to be nothing he could drink here. The lone stream he passed turned out to be dilute machine oil – and gritty. He had not realized how far they had come in the floater.

Despite his discomfort his mind kept circling back to the shining Jann. What a contrast – that marvellous ancient machine, compared to the cowardly little green robot! The operation had been successful, he thought wryly, but the patient died. The image of it tormented him – lying there, dying there, for lack of power. Had that been his service to it? Death in lieu of pain? 'O mortal,' it had pleaded, 'wouldst desert me . . .?' Yet he had left it.

But it wanted to kill him! He was lucky to have escaped with his life! He would be a fool ever to get near the ungrateful machine again!

That fading appeal nagged at him, even so.

Finally he reached the spaceport and staggered into the ALIEN LIFE SYSTEMS SUPPORT section. It was cramped and hot, but had the supplies he needed for the moment. He gulped water, then carefully bandaged his smarting feet. His job here was done.

Except for that last plea. . . .

'The Jann,' he inquired, not idly. 'What kind of moral

standards did they have? Did they ever make oaths, for instance, and keep them?'

The station's interior translator cleared its dusty speakers and answered him: 'The ancient Jann robots were compulsively moral, and were mighty oath makers. Their circuitry was so constructed that they were unable ever to reverse an oath once made, or to allow anything short of total incapacity to hinder its performance.'

So that was what he was up against!

But to let that noble creature simply lie there, knowing that not one of the frightened natives would help it. . . .

'What power source did the Jann employ?'

'They normally used a unique powerpack whose secret expired with them,' the translator said. 'A tiny unit would sustain them in full activity for many centuries. But in an emergency they were able to draw on almost any available source.'

Except sunlight, evidently, or radio waves, or the heat of the ground. Though perhaps such things had helped to recharge the Jann's unit, so that it could last forty centuries in spite of the short-circuit. 'How long before the next liner to the University of Dentistry, or that vicinity?'

'Eighteen hours, approximately.'

Time enough. 'Summon an individual floater for me, stocked with a spare charge-cell. I'll drive it myself.' He knew that his status as a representative from a Galactic University guaranteed his interplanetary credit. He could order virtually anything and have it delivered without challenge. If his charges became excessive, the University would settle without a whimper – and call him to account in private. That way its image was protected.

The floater was waiting outside as he eased himself along on his blisters. He mounted and set it in motion. The controls were standard.

In minutes he was back at the pit. The Jann lay where he had left it, spread unceremoniously face down. Its light glowed a trifle more brightly, however, suggesting that its cell had recharged a little. It might eventually have recovered enough power to crawl out by itself – were it not for the hazard of that temporary bridge he had installed.

Dillingham lifted out the charge-cell and set it beside the robot. 'I have brought you a temporary power supply,' he said. 'This is not to imply that I approve of your attitude, one bit – but it is against my principles to let any creature suffer or die if I am able to prevent it. So here is your reprieve – and by the time you hook it up and assemble it, I'll be gone. You'll have to find your own permanent supply, as I suspect this will sustain you only a few hours. Good luck.'

The Jann's shining hand dragged towards the cell, and Dillingham knew it would make use of that power somehow. He jumped into the floater and took off. 'None but I . . .' he heard as he left.

What kind of a fool *was* he? This Jann was murder! But he knew the answer: he was the same kind of fool who had thrown away his study-time in order to help a disreputable Oyster who claimed to be in pain. That had worked out well for him – but he could expect no similar reprieve this time. He was dealing with an inflexible machine, not a subjective animate, this time. He'd better be off the planet before the Jann got fully organized.

'None but I . . .'

Dillingham jumped, almost overturning the floater. He was a mile from the pit and travelling at high speed, yet it had sounded as though the Jann were near at hand. He looked around nervously.

'None but I shall do thee die.' It was the floater's transcoder!

He relaxed. Naturally the Jann would be able to tap into such a device. Its body was one big electronic apparatus.

'I see you're back in form already,' he replied.

'And my thanks to thee, mortal. For the second time thou hast preserved me from a fate forse than destruction. Thy primitive power cell is insufficient to sustain levitation, but I am now able to walk to a better supply. Then I shall seek thee out, for none but I shall—'

'I understand.' Levitation? The Jann *was* advanced; he had never heard of this ability in a robot, before. That probably meant the quaint-talking demon could catch him in the floater, or anywhere else on the planet. He suddenly felt less secure. In fact, something very like a chilly perspiration was showing up. 'How long will it take you to get better power?'

'There is a Jann unit in serviceable condition buried within ten miles of me. Twenty minutes will suffice, counting the time required to drill down to it. Then shall I be fully mobile again.'

Twenty minutes! His liner to the University wouldn't leave for many hours.

The spaceport was coming into sight, but this did not cheer him. Where could he hide from a virtually omniscient killer robot?

'Jann, are you sure you have to kill me?'

'Mortal, I must do thee die, for so I have sworn.'

'There's no leeway, no loophole—?'

'Only if thou shouldst die before I get to thee.'

'You couldn't just write this one off as a bad debt?'

'None but I—'

'I remember the expression.' But had there been a note of regret in it this time? 'I just thought the circumstances might—'

'Shall do thee die.' No – the tone was final.

Dillingham tried once more. 'Jann, your oath to kill your

142

benefactor was for the first time you were saved. Don't you owe me another oath for the second time?'

'I had not thought of it, mortal. I shall give thee the prior oath: to fulfill three wishes. That should acquit me honourably.'

'Excellent. My first wish is to cancel the other oath.'

There was something like a chuckle. 'Not so fast, mortal. Thou canst not gainsay a Jann oath in such fashion. Only after the first has been acquitted may thou invoke the next.'

'But how can I invoke – I mean, *revoke* it after I'm dead?'

'Mortal, I did not write the Code of the Jann; I only obey it. First oath first.'

So much for that. Dillingham drew up to the centre, paused a moment to collect his morale, and hurried to the ticket counter. 'Book me aboard the first ship out of here. Anywhere. Is there one within fifteen minutes?'

The blue robot with the rubber-stamp digits looked startled. 'Is something the matter, Director?'

'Your Jann wants to kill me.'

'That's too bad. We were afraid of something like that. Do you mind removing yourself from the building before the Jann catches up to you? We're not insured against acts of war.'

'Acts of war!'

'No peace treaty was ever concluded with the Jann, since we thought them extinct. So we're still at war. If it destroyed this station to get at you—'

Dillingham suspected it was useless to shout at a machine, but was tempted. 'Did it occur to you that the moment the Jann dispatches *me*, it will be free to resume full-scale hostilities against *you*? Now if you'd like me to go out to meet it—'

'Oh, no – it would be better if you lived for a while, at least until we can prepare our defences.'

'Just put me on a ship in time and you'll have no problem,' Dillingham said dryly. Who would have expected the quiet profession of prosthodontics to lead to this?

He found himself aboard a scow lurching off to Hazard, a planet devoted largely to winter sports for woolly mammoths. He didn't care; at least it had an up-to-date spaceport, and it would be a simple matter to re-embark for the University. Once home, he could check out ways to nullify the Jann, should it actually follow him into space.

But why wait? 'Creature-to-creature call to Director Oyster, School of Prosthodontics, University of Dentistry,' he said to the translator, and identified himself for the charges. That was one thing about the translators : they all seemed to know all languages, even his. Probably there was a complex network, so that—

'Good to hear you,' Oyster said. Even though this was a was a translation of a voice many light-years distant, the typical clammish nuances came through clearly. 'How soon will you be back?'

'Not soon enough, I'm afraid. You see, I'm headed in the wrong direction, and—'

A rough, somewhat nasal voice cut in. 'We demand grades based on longevity-in-programme, and tuition reduction for difficult courses. Furthermore—'

What was this – a crossed connection?

'Ridiculous !' Oyster exclaimed. 'I'll make you a counter-offer : longevity-in-programme based on your grades, and cessation of tuition after graduation. By that token you will soon wash out, Anteater, and the question of your graduation will be, if I may say so, academic.'

Anteater ! Dillingham recognized that voice now. His one-time room-mate had cheated on the University entrance exam, though he had hardly needed to. Now, evidently, he was leading a student revolt.

144

'Are you still there, Assistant?' Oyster inquired. 'They have us locked up in an examination room, and we need reinforcements.'

'Locked up! All your staff, too?'

'All that happened to be on the premises when they broke through. I'm here with Purplesplotch, K-9, Honeycomb and Lightbulb. I'm not sure you know them.'

'I remember Honeycomb. He was one of my AAC interviewers. That was an unforgettable—'

'We demand a full-credit sabbatical term every two years,' Anteater said.

'Sabbaticals! For *students*?' Oyster shouted back. 'Our budget doesn't allow that for our *instructors*! If you don't disperse this instant, though, I guarantee you'll get a term at full-labour in the University clink! Did you fix the Jann?'

Dillingham realized with a start that the last sentence was for him, and marvelled at Oyster's aplomb in this cross-fire dialogue. 'That's what I was calling about. The Jann is—'

'Hey! He's making an outside call!' another student cried. 'The no-good sneak!'

'Now wait a minute,' Dillingham began.

'That's *Earthman*!' Anteater said. 'I know him. A turncoat. Schemed his way into Administration after he'd flunked the entrance exam. Blank him off!'

'Clam chowder!' Oyster swore before Dillingham could reply. A red light flickered on the translator chassis to signify the transmission of an obscenity. 'Doctor, get back here as fast as you—'

'Oooo, what you said, Director!' Anteater chided gleefully. 'Did you hear that, fellows? He said "poisoned termites"!'

'Melted ice-cream!' another student echoed wickedly. 'Wash his mouth out!' Then the blah-blah of an interference signal over-rode the transmission and Dillingham could make out no more. He was on his own again.

He hardly had time to disconnect before the translator spoke again. 'None but I . . .'

Oh, no!

'So you can tap into a spaceborne network too, Jann. You're pretty good for one who's been buried four thousand years.'

'I have been keeping up with developments, primitive as they are, despite mine incapacity.'

'That's how you knew my language, without a translator? You rifled my transcoder electronically before I ever bridged your tooth?'

'Even so.'

'Then why don't you employ modern slang, instead of—'

'That would be out of character, mortal.'

'It seems out of character to me to kill the one who tried to help you. Twice. But I'm not a Jann, so maybe I don't properly appreciate your mores.'

'I shall await thee on Hazard.'

Dillingham felt distinctly uncomfortable. Even his feeble irony was wasted on the metal man, and now – 'You caught a faster ship?'

'I *am* a faster ship.'

Worse and worse. The long-range problem had become short-range again. He had assumed that 'levitation' was similar to the action of a floater, strictly dependent on adequate ambient gas – i.e., air. He had underestimated the robot.

He was tempted to ask the translator for advice, but realized that he could no longer trust it. Evidently his prior call had enabled the Jann to trace him, and now the robot would overhear anything he said. At worst, it might arrange to feed him false information, leading to the early fulfilment of the oath. He could not even converse with any crewman or other passengers, since translation would be necessary. He was boxed in, and would have to get out of it by himself. As usual.

But how? The Jann could track him whenever he used a translator or other communicator, and would be laying in wait for the ship at Hazard.

'With abilities such as yours, how did your kind lose the war?' Dillingham inquired. Since he could not hide from the giant, he might as well talk. There was always the chance that something useful would turn up, that would enable him to circumvent the murder-oath. A straw – but he had little else.

'I have pondered that very question for some centuries,' the Jann admitted. 'Unfortunately, we of the mineral kingdom are not original thinkers, so I was unable to come to any certain conclusion.'

Not original thinkers. That figured. A machine typically performed as instructed and had no imagination. But that realization only posed more problems. How could an entire machine culture evolve, without animate intervention? If one of its highest representatives, the Jann, could neither win a war nor comprehend why it had lost, what was the source of its civilization?

On the other hand, was his own planet dominated by original thinkers? 'Were you able to come to any *un*certain conclusions?' Dillingham asked.

'I conjectured that we Jann, being advanced and peaceful, did not properly appreciate the capacity for an inferior species to do mischief. We believed that all robots shared our standards. So when we were attacked—'

'I had understood that *you* were the aggressors.'

'No, mortal. We governed the planet, and all other planets in a range of an hundred light-years, as we had for many millenia. We had no need of violence. It was our lesser mechanicals – smaller robots we built as domestics and functionaries – who rebelled. Before we fully appreciated the extent of their dastardy, we were undone.'

That was a different story from the one the contemporar
robots told, yet it could be the truth. Winners always di
paraged the motives and characters of the losers. The Jan
did appear to be a superior species, and it was more likel
that the Jann could build lesser robots than that the lesse
ones could build Jann. Except—

'If you built the other robots, who built *you*?'

'We evolved, mortal. Natural selection—'

'Surely you don't, well, breed? How can you evolve th
way animals do?'

'I never understood how the animals perform. No tool
no charts, no preparations. Just a brief physical contact, le:
even than an exchange of lubrication. Very untechnologica
Quite sloppy, in fact, I once watched—'

'Never mind that. What about your own romantic life?

There was a pause. When the Jann spoke again, its voic
was subdued. 'How well do I remember my Janni, her limb
of shining platinum, her teeth of iridium . . . and the little on
we built together, pride of my nut and screw. My chart an
hers, distinct but compatible. We knew the cross betwee
the two designs would generate a superior being, a machin
like none before. But then the rebellion erupted, and Jann
was melted in an atomic furnace, and our son dismantled fc
parts for the usurper, whilst I lay helpless in the pit. . . .'

Dillingham did not know what to say. This Jann, far fro
being a mindless monster, was as meaningful a personality a
any true sentient. Were it not for that oath—

Static burst from the translator. What now?

It subsided after a few seconds. 'Ah, mortal, why did
not heed thy warning!' the Jann exclaimed.

'Because your caution-circuit has been bridged out.'

'Vicious circle. The cold of space has fractured that bridg
and in a moment my tooth—'

More static. Dillingham realized that fate had given hi

yet another chance. The Jann would be immobilized again, this time in deep space.

'Farewell, mor—' but static cut off the rest. The cold had completed its work, and the intermittent failure had become permanent.

Dillingham sat for half an hour in silence, listening to the continuing static. He knew that every minute of it meant a minute of terrible suffering for the Jann. Unless something were done, the robot would drift through space forever, in an agony it hardly deserved.

Yet his own life was sweet, and he had a promising future. Should he throw it all away . . . again?

'Clam chowder!' he said at last. Then he put through a call to the spaceport at Hazard. 'A derelict is moving in your direction, and should pass within the range of your landing net in the next few hours. Intercept it and perform the following repair.' He went on to describe the tooth-bridging operation. 'And locate an appropriate replacement for the affected tooth, if you can, because there is an important circuit involved.'

'It shall be done, Director,' the official said. 'Where do you want the ship delivered after it has been repaired?'

'It isn't a ship, exactly. It's a self-propelled robot. Let it go when you're through and charge the service to my University account.'

'Very well, Director.' The official signed off.

Once a fool, always a fool, he thought. He simply could not preserve his own life at the cost of eternal torture for another creature, even an inanimate one. He wanted to live, certainly – but the end did not justify the means.

That was hardly an attitude, he thought ruefully, that a creature like Anteater would comprehend. Dillingham hardly comprehended it himself. Probably Anteater would outlive him. . . .

At any rate, he had a reprieve of a few hours, unless they repaired the Jann before Dillingham reached Hazard himself. He would have to gamble on getting in and out before the pursuit resumed. He still could not use the translator, because he knew the Jann was listening in even though it could not reply or act. Better to swear off such devices entirely, so that at least he would be hidden.

But he was still bottled in. He could not get off the ship before it landed, and once it *did* land. . . .

Then he remembered the lifeboats. How could he call the Jann an unoriginal thinker, when that escape had almost bypassed his own mental circuitry !

Dillingham drew out some thin paperlike dental illustrations and began to draw on their blank backs. He took some pains, erasing frequently and redrawing. He wound up with several complex configurations.

He left the compartment silently, using the emergency manual door control. He searched out the Captain's cabin. He used his knuckles to knock on the door, avoiding the electronic signaller. Then he stepped back so as to be out of range of the viewscreen pick-up. He could, however, still see the screen's projected image.

The screen came on and the Captain's whiskery proboscis showed. There were sounds indicating a question. Since the hall translator had no object to fix on, it had to feed through the Captain's native speech. Translators could perform moderat linguistic miracles, but were not equipped to play guessing games among the several million discreet galactic languages.

Dillingham did not answer. Any word he said would be relayed straight to the Jann as well as to the Captain.

After a moment the screen snapped off. False alarm, the Captain had evidently decided. Such things happened on old ships. Then Dillingham went up to tap on the door again.

After several repeats, the frustrated Captain opened the

door personally to investigate the nature of the malfunction. Dillingham poked one of his ornate symbol-signs around the corner.

The officer paused, making no sound. Here was the test: would he understand? He commanded a broken-down vessel and was largely over the hill himself – but that should mean the Captain had had over a century of experience. He must have knocked about the galaxy considerably. Such a creature should know the galactic graphics shorthand.

The GG shorthand was a system of symbols based on meaning, not phonics. Just as the Chinese written language of Earth could be used by those speaking a number of dissimilar dialects and languages, because each figure stood for a specific concept and not a spoken word – in just this way the galactic shorthand was a universal written language. Any creature of the galaxy who could see at all – and most could – was able to learn to read the symbols. The basic vocabulary was designed to apply even to languages that did not employ verbs, nouns and other familiar parts of speech. (In fact, the majority did not; Dillingham's own family of languages represented an archaic fluke, as far as the galaxy was concerned.)

But not every individual bothered to master the shorthand. In fact, few other than travelling scholars retained proficiency in it, though every University had a mandatory freshman course in it. Translators and transcoders were ubiquitous, so the written art languished – particularly since there were also translators for written material that were just as efficient as the verbal ones.

Dillingham was gambling that the Captain had had to poke into so many backward planets that the shorthand would have been a useful and necessary tool. Dillingham was also gambling that his own just-completed freshman course had made him proficient enough to be intelligible. He had been instructed by drugs and suggestion, and really could not be certain how much or how well he knew.

The Captain angled one eye-stalk around the corner. Below this floating eyeball was a tentacle looped around an old-fashioned short-range blaster – the type of weapon useful for wiping out opposition without puncturing any vital pipes. The charge could burn off Dillingham's clothing and hair and epidermis quickly, and kill him slowly. He stood absolutely still.

The Captain came around the corner and gestured down the hall. Dillingham marched as directed. No other communication occurred. Had the creature understood?

They entered a blank cold cubicle. A single neon cast an eerie light on the single locked file-cabinet. This was an ancient ship, to have equipment like this! The Captain drew out a genuine physical metal key and unlocked the cabinet. He withdrew a bundle of cards. His tentacles riffed through them before selecting one. He held it up.

It was a symbol in the shorthand, neatly printed. It said: JANN.

The Captain understood! The sharp old codger had already divined Dillingham's problem. He must have made an inquiry at Metallica, being too canny to accept a passenger without knowing exactly why the creature could not afford to wait for a better ship.

Dillingham's first symbol had been the code for EMERGENCY, modified by a qualifier requesting that no overt acknowledgement be made. It was essentially a wartime symbol, intended for use by a spy in enemy territory when open communication could mean discovery and rapid oblivion. (There must have been interesting chapters in galactic history!) It was quite out of place in an old vessel on a milk-run – but the experienced Captain had put one and one together successfully.

The rest was easy. The Captain named a figure for putting the fugitive ashore in a lifeboat, and Dillingham agreed though the price seemed high. The Captain then took him to an airlock and installed him in a tiny compartment. The creature saw that he was securely strapped down, then punched a destination without using the translator. So far so good – since no communications equipment had been used the Jann should have no idea what Dillingham was doing.

But by the same token, Dillingham had no certain notion where the Captain was sending him.

The airlock closed, sealing him off. There was a rough lurch as the lifeboat detached itself, then a feeling of tremendous weight as its antique chemical rockets blasted. He was on his way.

Now that it was too late to change his mind it occurred to him that it would have been easy for the Captain to route the lifeboat into nowhere, claiming that it was suicide while collecting the University remittance. . . .

No! The University would automatically challenge any payment to be made under suspicious circumstances, and the Captain would be well aware of that. Foul play would be far more trouble than it was worth.

Anyway, the Captain had an honest snout.

Dillingham did not dare turn on the viewscreen to see where he was going, because the Jann could probably tap into that too. He had to go blind, hoping that he was losing the robot as effectively as he was confusing himself.

Time passed, and he slept, while the boat sailed on. It was in free-fall now; but he was not : the rotating hull provided partial weight. He dreamed of scintillating living machines with glowing teeth.

The braking rockets jolted him into uncomfortable awareness. He was almost there. He hoped it was a civilized planet. Otherwise he had merely traded one demise for another.

It was a cruel landing. When the pressure and furore subsided and he regained consciousness, he struggled into a suit and cranked open the port. He still did not dare to use the powered equipment, for that would have required instruction over the translator. He was prepared to face a blizzard or an inferno or solid water or. . . .

He was disappointed. This was plainly the landscape of Metallica.

What had he really expected? Obviously the spaceship had not gone far in the short time he had been aboard. Naturally the lifeboat, being chemically underpowered, had taken much longer to traverse the same distance. Probably most of its thrust had been used merely to reverse the initial inertia. The closest planet had to be the one he had just left, for space was large.

And where was the Jann now? By this time the repair should have been completed. . . .

He smiled. The super-robot would be on Hazard, wondering what had become of a certain dentist.

Dillingham contemplated the countryside. This was not the same section of the planet where he had found the Jann. The vegetation here was more richly metallic, the flower-filaments more brilliant, the green-copper lichen more abundant, the oil streamlet ungritty. There were rust-capped mountains, and a valley serviced by a bubbling diesel-fuel lake. And no sign of civilization.

In short, an unspoiled wilderness area.

All very good. The Jann would eventually figure out the truth and come jetting back to Metallica, but would hardly find him here. A planet was too big to search in a hurry. He had scrupulously operated no electronic equipment, so it could not trace him that way.

Meanwhile, he had merely to avoid starvation.

Behind him the lifeboat translator crackled into life, though he had not turned it on. 'None but I . . .'

Dillingham sighed. That was another talent he hadn't known about. The Jann could not only tap into communicatins, it could operate them remotely. Thus it had established its rapport with the lifeboat translator, and would home in on that.

That simple!

'How long before you get here?' he inquired with prickly resignation. The robot must have obtained the registry of the lifeboat and learned the frequency of its translator, so that—

'Seventeen minutes, mortal. Take care that no harm befall thee in the interim, for I would suffer sorely were mine oath abridged.'

'Thine oath be damned!' Dillingham shouted, and immediately wondered whether he could accomplish anything by threatening suicide. Probably not, since the robot would check it out before indulging in other pursuits. Anyway, he'd have to write out a Last Will & Testament specifying what his three wishes were, for the sake of the second oath, and the disposition of the wealth owing from the third oath. Assuming it worked that way. The money could go to a dental research foundation back on Earth, and the three wishes – would Miss Galland appreciate three robotic wishes? It was all too complicated.

Seventeen minutes, ticking away already. Such a short time to hide himself in this brush, away from the lifeboat. And he'd better dispose of his University transcoder, too. Unless he wanted to stay and face down the Jann. . . .

Useless: a machine could not be bluffed. On the other hand, if he did succeed in eluding it, what would he gain? A tedious expiration from hunger and thirst?

Opposing the thing physically was out of the question.

He was forty-two years old, and had never been the robust type.

His only real chance was to outsmart it. For all its talents, it did not seem to be particularly bright, or he would never have escaped it this long. It could easily have interfered with the lifeboat's guidance system and made it crash, for example. had it figured out where he was soon enough. Or prevented him from ever boarding the scow to Hazard, by fouling up the spaceport translators. It had missed marvellous opportunities.

Also, it seemed to feel obliged to answer all questions put to it. That was another machine trait. Probably it was incapable of lying, or of evading the truth, unlike the inferior contemporary robots. That could be its weakness.

'Why didn't you foul up the spaceport's communications network, to prevent me from leaving Metallica?' he asked. Maybe if he probed enough—

'That would have interfered with thy freedom of motion.'

'What do you care about that, since you intend to kill me anyway?'

'The rights of a sentient creature may not be voided, unless directly contrary to a specific Jann oath. So it is recorded, so must it be. Wherever thou art, there will I find thee, and there will I do thee die. Then will I grant thee three wishes, for the second time thou savest me—'

'And then enrich me forever and ever, for the third time. I know.'

'Then only will the oaths be acquitted, and I free.'

This didn't seem to be getting him anywhere. He already knew the robot was impervious to irony about the feasibility of the remaining boons after the first had been accomplished. Probably there were Jann statutes to cover the situation even if he never mentioned the oaths in his will.

There were only about ten minutes left. His stomach felt

like a sponge full of pepper-sauce, and his brain was not too clear. He was sure that he would rest easier if he simply accepted what was to be, but his innards wouldn't co-operate.

'How can I stop you from killing me?' he blurted.

'I may not tell thee that, mortal, for it would violate the letter of mine oath.'

'So there *is* a way!'

'I refuse to answer, on the grounds that it might tend to compromise mine oath, or lead in some devious way to—'

'Oh shut up!' Why had he bothered to try? Even the Jann's archaic affectations were irritating; he was sure the machine was not consistent in this speech.

But there was a way! The Jann had tried to evade the issue, but had bungled it. If only he could figure out the loophole, or trick the machine into telling him. Perhaps it *wanted* to tell him, but was prevented by its metallic code of ethics.

He needed time to think. He had barely five minutes left, but if he managed to hide, he might have a couple of days before the end. Maybe growing hunger would sharpen his imagination.

The lifeboat had a supply of water. Dillingham drank until he bulged, looked for a container to carry some with him, and finally set off frustrated. No time! The brush was thick, out beyond the section the rockets had blasted clear. A number of flower filaments gave off heat, which was another break. The Jann would have a tough time picking him out by body-warmth.

He heard a peculiar swish in the direction of the lifeboat and couldn't resist looking back. Sure enough, the Jann was coming down, resplendent in the sunlight. It was vertical, descending feet-first, like a shining god. No jets were visible.

To think that this thing had been built by loving mechanical parents before true civilization ever evolved on Earth! And it was still far ahead of anything Earth science knew. Yet it was determined to kill the man who had saved it three times. . . .

He broke from his reverie and moved on, carefully but quickly. He hoped the Jann was not equipped to sniff out his trail, like a bloodhound.

Evidently it wasn't, for he could hear it casting about in the wrong direction. He had been smart to divest himself of his last communications item. Then the Jann appeared in the sky again, swinging around a pinkish beam of light.

Dillingham ducked behind a humming iron tree until the way was clear. A beam that was visible in broad daylight was probably well worth avoiding.

A noise snapped his attention to the ground. There was an animal: a robot-beast. Its scales were burnished copper, its teeth stainless steel, its eyes white-hot filaments. He hardly had time to marvel that it should so strongly resemble an Earthly carnivore, before it sprang.

He dodged instinctively and caught hold of an aluminium sapling to pull himself away. The creature ground gears with a hungry roar and spun about as it touched ground, but its momentum prevented it from leaping again immediately. It had little wheels where foot-pads would have been on a living predator, and shock absorbers in the ankles.

What possible use would it have for his alien flesh! But he dived for a larger trunk and scrambled up its knobby bark as the beast came at him. Now he regretted imbibing all that water! He was weak and heavy, and he sloshed inside. But the thing chasing him was, after all, an animal, and probably attacked anything that invaded its hunting-ground – even though a single bite of Dillingham should foul its gears and rust its tongue.

The jaws snapped just beneath him and a jet of hot air scorched his posterior. The animal's air-cooling, probably –

but it was reminiscent of eager breath. He climbed another two feet – then stiffened.

Wire tendrils were dropping on him from the tree's tinsel foliage. They coiled like corkscrews, and a slickness glistened on their points. Acid, surely. . . .

Below, the animal opened its jaws. Dillingham could see right down its throat. The effect was that of a sausage-grinder.

He was trapped. The first tree-wire touched his head, and he smelled burning hair and felt a sharp pain as though a magnifying glass were focused on that spot. He jerked away – towards the grinning beast.

'Help!' he cried, not caring how inane it sounded or how useless it was.

And the Jann came.

In seconds it whistled through the brush and landed beside the tree. A lance of fire from its chest melted the face of the predator. Ear-splitting sonics from its head caused the tree's wires to retreat hastily. 'None but I shall do thee die!' the Jann bellowed.

It reached for Dillingham. He closed his eyes, knowing the end had come. Metal pincers closed on his body, lifted. For a moment he dangled; then he felt the ground under his feet.

Dillingham stumbled as the robot let go. 'I wish you'd get it over with,' he said, now oddly calm.

'First must I grant thee one token boon, before I do thee die. Thou must needs make thy request within fifteen seconds, according to Jannish custom.' It began ticking, one tick per second, as though it were a metronome. Or a bomb.

Fifteen seconds to come up with that loophole, when he hadn't been able to do it in the past day! Ten seconds, and the Jann was aiming its chest-nozzle at him. Five, and his mind was numb. . . .

'A postponement!' he cried, half facetiously.

'Granted,' the Jann said. 'How long?'

Ah, foolishness. 'Fifty years!'

He waited for the derisive bolt of heat, but it didn't come. 'Granted, mortal.'

Dillingham stared. 'You mean – you'll wait?'

It almost seemed that the metal face was smiling. The mouth was open, at any rate, and the gleaming new tooth was visible. Apparently the Hazard spaceshop had stocked the item, restoring the caution-circuit. 'Originally I contemplated a shorter period, but I perceived that this would be an injustice. Thou art not the fortune-hunter I expected, nor yet the fool I suspected. And we Jann are not unmindful of honest courtesies rendered.'

Dillingham was abruptly reminded of Oyster, whose mode of operation had a certain similarity to this. He hoped he never encountered another such personality. 'So you modified the spirit of the oath slightly,' he suggested, 'if not the letter.'

'Our oaths are always subject to interpretation,' the Jann agreed. 'I could not tell thee, but I delayed for a time, that thou shouldst realize it for thyself. None but I shall do thee die : no animal, no entity, no microbe, no act of nature. But it shall be a kind demise, and it shall come in exactly fifty years, as thou requesteth. I shall always be near thee, to see that mine oath is honoured.'

So the Jann had become a bodyguard, perhaps the most competent in all the galaxy, preserving him from all perils until he was ninety-two. Just a tiny shift in interpretation, and the oath had swung from negative to positive.

'That tooth – did it contain your compassion-circuit, too?' he asked, suddenly catching on.

'Even so, mortal.'

'Well come on, Jann,' Dillingham cried, remembering something. 'We have a student strike to deal with, back at the University. Oyster will kill me if I don't manage to relieve the siege before all his files are gone!'

CHAPTER SEVEN

'Now here is the problem of your contract,' Trach said. 'Gleep transferred it to Ra, so—'

Judy was almost convinced that Trach was not the monster he appeared. He had not, after all, eaten her when he had the opportunity, and certainly he was the essence of politeness. He claimed to be a vegetarian reptile, and if he were not fattening her up for a later feast. . . .

'Does that mean it *wasn't* a mistake? The trolls – my being on the—?'

'They don't make mistakes of that nature,' he said reassuringly. 'You are on their list.'

'To die in the radium mines?' Maybe it would be preferable to be eaten by a dinosaur ! 'How could the muck-a-muck do such a terrible thing? I trusted him to help me !'

'Merely good business practice. Nothing personal. He wouldn't be muck-a-muck if he wasted Gleep's credit status. Fifty pounds of frumpstiggle—'

'He told me a hundred !' she said indignantly.

'That was to improve your self-image. It was his impression that you were overly dependent on Dr. Dillingham and lacked confidence in your own dental abilities.'

'But I'm *not* a dentist ! I can't do prosthodontic—'

'Pretty sharp judge of character, that muck-a-muck. You *do* lack confidence.'

'Oh, shut up !'

'At any rate, he *did* help you. He notified me, knowing that I would arrange something. That's my business, after all – arranging things for mutual profit and my own. Unfortunately—'

'You don't have fifty pounds of frumpstiggle?'

'As a matter of fact, I have considerably more, thanks to a generous settlement on Dr. Dillingham and a successful mission at Electrolus. But—'

'But—?'

'But the trolls of Ra are very fussy about allowing any entity to depart. Once they hold a contract—'

'They won't let go,' she finished grimly.

'Not readily. Others in the galaxy have some very ugly suspicions about Ra. If too many prospective miners were to be released, those suspicions would be amply confirmed. Then it would be almost impossible for Ra to buy up contracts, at any price, and there could be galactic lawsuits for Ra's violation of contractee rights. There might even be an AUP quarantine for industrial malpractice, and *that* would finish Ra.'

'AUP?'

'Association of University Presidents. Very potent.'

'I see. So I have to take up pick and shovel?'

'Oh, no. They are very efficient here. You would work in your speciality, caring for the miners' teeth. Better dentures allow them to consume cruder staples, and that is more economical, you see.'

'I see again. I don't approve the motive, though.'

'Appreciation of Ra motives is an acquired taste. In certain respects, there is more need here for medical and dental assistants than for full MDs or DDSs, because only short-term measures are economical. The radiation, you know. And you would still be exposed to that.'

She nodded. Had she really thought her prospects back on Earth bad?

'I have not relinquished the problem, Miss Galland. I merely wish you to comprehend its magnitude. Naturally we'll find a way to remove you from Ra.'

'I comprehend the magnitude. What do I have to do, to escape?'

'You have to obtain a sponsor who is able to influence the troll hierarchy. I can arrange temporary reprieve, but my influence is limited. I'm only a diplomat. If I push my luck—'

'The mines for you too,' she said. 'Will you teach the prisoners diplomacy as they perish from radiation?'

'I doubt it would come to that, but there could be awkwardness. However, I'll see what I can do. I have had experience at a number of influential courts.'

Judy smiled appreciatively, but she had little hope.

Trach had been unduly modest about his resources. Within six hours there was an urgent call from the Monarch of Lepidop: he wanted an experienced dental assistant and he wanted this particular one. Since his subjects were resistive to radium poisoning, a task force of his navy traditionally transported Ra's annual output of ten pounds pure to the galactic markets.

He had, in short, influence.

The troll hierarchy swallowed its gall and hastily made a gift of Judy's contract to the Monarch, compliments of the honourable reputation of Ra. To make it quite clear where she had come from, they decided to brand her first. Of course, if she were willing to swear never to reveal what she had seen planetside, even this small formality might be dispensed with. . . .

Judy contemplated the sizzling branding iron, thought about the difficulty she would have sitting down thereafter, and saw her courage go up in steam. She agreed not to talk.

Then the troll released her hair and she fell to the floor.

Trach took her to Lepidop himself. This was a favour she appreciated less than she might have, for his ship was a frightening rattletrap. But she suspected that this was Trach's way of saving his own reptilian hide, for the trolls of Ra surely were aware of his part in Lepidop's demand, and would not delay unduly in attempting to resettle the score. Nice world, Ra.

Lepidop, in contrast, was truly beautiful. Iridescent films decorated its aesthetic continents, and rainbows were reflected from its shining oceans.

The ship jolted to rest on a platform mounted on a spire about two miles above the surface. July was afraid the weight of the ship would collapse the insubstantial edifice, but there was no sag or tremor. They emerged to meet the Lepidops.

'Butterflies!' Judy exclaimed. 'What marvellous wings!'

'This is Lepidop,' Trach reminded her gently. 'Capital world of the declining Lepidopteran Empire. But you are right to compliment their wings: Leps are subject to flattery. Now the honour guard will insist on conveying you personally to the Monarch, and I don't see how you can refuse.'

'An honour guard? I'm the one who's flattered! And I want to thank the Monarch effusively for saving me from Ra. Why should I refuse?'

'Well, their mode of transportation is not to every creature's taste. I would prefer to walk, myself. But since I am not permitted within the palace environs, I shall merely relay my compliments and depart for my next mission.'

'You're going?' Her original distrust of him was as though it had never been. Trach was as nice a dinosaur as she had ever met. 'I thought—'

'Some of the finer architectural structures are delicate, and I'm rather solid,' he explained. An understatement; she judged he weighed several tons. 'But the Monarch is basically a kindly fellow; don't let his gruffness fool you. And beware of palace intrigues. I'm sure he'll treat you well, provided—'

'But how do I find Dr. Dillingham?'

'I'll notify the University of Dentistry. They'll advise him in due course. You just stay put and wait for word. It may take a while.'

She had other questions, suddenly pressing now that Trach was about to leave her. But the man-sized butterflies were upon them, a fluttering phalanx. 'Provided *what?*' she whispered urgently.

'Miss Earthbiped?' a translator inquired. She didn't see the instrument, but hardly needed to. There was always a translator within earshot on civilized planets, except for places like Gleep where such machinery was inconvenient, and Enen, where they couldn't afford the expense. She automatically associated the translation with the speaker, as she had once associated sub-titles with foreign speech in Earth movies.

'This is Miss Galland of Earth,' Trach said formally. She had to pick up the introduction through the translator, for he was speaking directly in Lepidopteran. He was a phenomenal linguist! 'Summoned by the Monarch, for dental assistancy and hygiency.' And privately to her: 'Provided he lives.'

'This way, honoured guest,' the lead butterfly said, spreading his huge yellow wings as he turned. Judy followed him to an ornate and fragile little cage. the other butterflies falling in around her and matching her step. 'Enter the royal carriage.'

She hesitated, the Ra experience fresh in her memory. This thing had neither wheels nor runners, and white bars encircled it. It reminded her of a lobster trap. But Trach gave her a thumbs-up signal from across the platform, and she had to trust him again. She opened the latticed gate and climbed in.

The fit was tight, vertically, and there was no proper seat; evidently this had been designed for a reclining butterfly. A arrow section of the top was peaked: space for folded wings to project.

The yellow butterfly closed the gate with one of his six small legs. She arranged herself half-supine, propped against one elbow so she could wave to Trach. Then the others circled the cage, picked up threads hanging from its sides, and beat the white wings in unison while the yellow called the cadence.

'Hup! Two! Three! Four!' she heard, not certain whether there was a translator, or at least a little transcoder in the cage, or whether her own mind was doing it. 'Hup! . . . Hup! . . .'

Suddenly they were aloft: butterflies, cage and Judy – clinging desperately to the bars. No wonder Trach had been nervous about the transportation. But it was too late to protest now.

They flew over the edge of the platform, and she closed her eyes to stop the vertigo. Two miles in the air – with only butterfly wings and slender threads to support her! Did the Monarch often travel this way? Was that what Trach had meant by his hasty warning: the Monarch would treat her well, provided he lived? Let one thread snag, one wing falter. . . .

But the cadence was steady, and she was reassured that they were not about to drop her. She watched the aerial life of Lepidop: brown-winged butterflies, grey ones, green ones and blue, gliding their myriad ways. A number carried bags in two or three hands, as though they had been shopping, and others clustered and whirled in dazzling mid-air games.

Yet Trach had said the Lepidopteran Empire was declining.

The palace was a tremendous silken nest, with massed strands forming gleaming geometric patterns that glowed prismatically in the slanting sunlight. At every nexus a pastel-winged butterfly perched, gently fanning the air. 'Air conditioning!' she murmured.

The cage came to rest in a cushiony chamber, and the bearers let go the threads. Judy disembarked cautiously, and found the seemingly tenuous webbing quite strong. It gave little under her feet, adding bounce to her step, and was in fact rather fun to walk on. Trach would have put a foot through, however.

The yellow butterfly led the way to the throne room. This was a splendid chamber whose lofty arches reached into a nebulous web-flung dome and whose furniture was all of stressed silk. Upon the mighty yet delicate throne reclined the ruler of the planet and empire.

The Monarch was old. His torso was stiff and scaley, his antennae drooped, and his wings were dead white cardboard. Had he been human, she would have assessed his age at an infirm eighty. She knew immediately that he had no teeth.

Why, then, had he wanted a dental assistant? Had his demand been made purely as a favour to Trach, or was there more to it?

'My dear, come here,' the Monarch whispered, and the translator conveyed jointly benign and imperative tonality.

She stepped up to him, impressed by his bearing despite his antiquity. It was no longer a mystery why Trach had been concerned for the Monarch's life. It was as though the very act of speaking might terminate his span.

'You care for teeth?'

'Yes, Your Majesty,' she replied, deciding not to quibble over descriptions. She was no dentist, but she *did* take care of teeth.

'You have experience with—' here he paused to regain his shallow breath. 'Lepidop mandibulars?'

'On my world, butterflies don't have teeth.'

'Interesting. On Lepidop (another breath), *primates* don't'

168

have teeth.' He laughed – a painful rattle, even in translation. 'But I suppose you (breath) don't have genuine lepids, any (breath) more than we have real primates. (Breath, breath) It is merely a con (breath) venience of expression.'

Judy was happy to agree. This royal butterfly had no connection to any Earthly creature, just as Judy Galland had no connection to any galactic biped. The Monarch was not stupid, but he was rapidly weakening from the effort of conversation. Gruffness was hardly the problem; a fatal oversociability might be.

'Dismissed,' the Monarch snapped.

Two small purple Leps hurried her out of the chamber. 'He's obnoxious when balked,' one confided to her. 'But he'll die soon, fortunately,' the other said.

This irritated her unreasonably. 'Now stop that! I think he's very nice, and I won't have you saying such things behind his back.'

The butterflies tittered, and she realized that she had chosen a poor figure of speech that the translator had rendered literally. There was no 'behind' for a butterfly's back; there was only 'above'. And that ruined the sentiment. She had made a fool of herself to no purpose. Their remarks might even have been well intentioned – and were probably true.

Well, Trach had told her to beware of palace intrigues. She had probably already put her foot in it by speaking out thoughtlessly. She would be more careful henceforth.

They showed her to a private chamber without further comment and left her. There was a galactic all-purpose unit that took care of all conceivable and some inconceivable physical needs, and she had learned how to squeeze entertainment from a standard translator. 'Sing me a ballad,' she directed it. And it did.

The Monarch summoned her to another audience next

day. He was considerably more affable, and she suspected that the court minions had dutifully relayed her remarks to him. She had spoken automatically, but she had defended the Monarch. Had she been negatively impressed, she might have said something entirely different, with no more thought. Or just let it pass. Little accidents like this could make all the difference, as she knew from her experience with patients on Earth. That was one reason dental assistants were usually personable and cautious about giving opinions. Usually.

Now she almost felt guilty for speaking out, as though she had deliberately played politics. Maybe, subconsciously she had.

But still the Monarch had no teeth, so could have no use for her. She was embarrassed, holding her little case of instruments. What politics was *he* playing?

'My dear, I like your spirit. (Breath) Most visitors praise me lavishly (breath) to my antennae, but sneer (breath) behind their wings. How would (breath) you like to visit my past?'

'Your Majesty, I don't understand.'

'I am forty-two years old,' he said. The translator had rendered the time span into her terms, just as the all-purpose unit had created light and darkness to match her Earthly pattern of day and night. But it was a surprise. The Monarch was just about the same age as Dr. Dillingham ! 'We Lepids have lesser lifespans (breath) than some of you landbound forms. But then we (breath) have greater abilities. So life is fair.'

She had little basis to object, yet the Monarch's abilities were obviously long past. 'I don't know how to – to visit your past. I'm sorry.'

'Of course you don't, my dear. (Breath) I shall take you. Ten years; I (breath) have strength enough for that.'

Whatever it was, if it required strength it was best discouraged. He could afford no superfluous expenditures of energy. 'I don't see what this has to do with dental hygiene, Your Majesty. Why take *me*?'

'Give me your hand,' the Monarch said. 'Oh, you have only two. (Breath) Awkward, but I suppose you're used to it.'

'Yes.' Hesitantly she held out one of her few hands, and he took it with one of his stick-thin members. His grasp was so feeble that she was afraid to close her fingers; even her lightest grip might crush his chitinous appendage.

He shuddered. Something like a mild shock went up her arm. Then there was a strange shimmer. A wave of dizziness passed over her.

'Ten years,' the Monarch said with pride. 'My subjects can manage no more than five, even in their primes.'

She disengaged her hand from his surprisingly strong grip and looked at him, wondering whether he could be senile. A decade could not be wished away.

His wings were orange. His body was full. His antennae were erect. He looked twenty years younger.

Judy felt strange. Her clothing did not fit comfortably. Her blouse was loose, her skirt tight, her shoes wrong. She felt gangling and her face itched. What was wrong?

'And now I have my teeth again,' he said, smiling. And he did. 'Of course they are not in good condition, and in five more years I lost them entirely. But with your care and advice I may be able to preserve them longer.'

This seemed to answer an important question, but she hardly heard him. 'I'm younger too!' she exclaimed.

'Naturally. So is the palace, the planet, the galaxy. This is my past.'

'Time travel? That's impossible!'

'Impossible for you, certainly. And for most species. That is why I was able to extend my empire so readily, though it is drifting away now that my powers have declined.'

'But what about paradox? I mean—'

'There is no conflict. We are ten years younger, and the universe is ten years younger, but we are not of it, precisely. The full explanation would be too technical for your comprehension. We merely experience, we do not affect, except for our own bodies.'

Judy shook her head. 'How could you conquer an empire if you couldn't use your talent to affect it?'

'Simple. I travel to a foreign planet, then I visit its past and make notes. Then I comprehend its vulnerability, and in the present I exploit it. No enemy strategy is a surprise to me, nor can it ever be, unless it dates from beyond my own lifetime.'

'Your Majesty, it still doesn't make sense. I see you younger, and I seem to be about sixteen myself. But when I was really sixteen I was a high-school girl on Earth, ruining my teeth with cola. So this can't be—'

'It is my past, my dear, not yours. You become younger merely to stay in phase with me. I would take you to Earth and show you that school, of yours, but my migrating years are over and no ship will respond to our touch now. You may look at Lepidop instead.'

'Don't tell me you migrated between planets without ships!'

'Don't tell you? Very well, you shall remain ignorant of that talent.' The Monarch preceded her to a silken parapet walling off a bulging room, so that they actually stood outside the body of the castle. Beyond it the colourful butterflies danced in the early dusk, whirling in columns of turbulence. 'See, the chrono gives the date,' he said, gesturing towards a huge clock-tower about a mile distant. 'Just over ten years ago.'

She was the clock but did not know how to read its symbols. She was coming to believe that they had travelled back;

nothing else explained the phenomena. She *was* younger; she could not be deceived about a thing like that. The Monarch now had plenty of breath and physical vigour, and he *did* have remarkable powers.

A yellow messenger lighted on the parapet. July stepped back, but the insect took no note of her or the Monarch. The yellow mouth parts were moving, but she heard no translation. Naturally not, she realized when she considered it: the machines could not have been programmed for English ten years before she came. They would be inoperative for her – and of course unnecessary for the natives.

Then how, she wondered sharply, was she able to hear and comprehend the Monarch's present speech?

'My dear,' he remarked, 'your thought processes are so delightfully open. The phase applies to the translators too, but only for you and me. We cannot communicate with the creatures of this time, or indeed make ourselves known to them in any way. I heard no more than you did, just then.'

'Oh,' she said, more perplexed than ever.

A thick-bodied, furry antennaed drab moth arrived on foot. It gazed out over the parapet a moment as though envious of the aerial ceremonies beyond, then lowered its head to the wall. A tremendous tongue uncurled and brushed the tight strands that formed the parapet and all the castle/palace. She saw with shock that its wings had been partially clipped, so that it could not fly.

'The menials come out at night,' the Monarch murmured distastefully. 'We don't associate with them, of course, but we recognize that they do have to clean the grounds *sometime*.'

'The moths? They do the work?'

'That is the natural order, since they are basically inferior. We merely relieve them of the onus of making decisions. No doubt they are happier than we are.'

The moth hardly looked happy. It seemed resigned, feeling no frustration, apart from that one glance outside, because it had no hope. She started to voice a protest at this callousness of the Monarch, but he spoke first: 'We'll return to the throne-room. You shall instruct me on caring for my teeth.'

That was right – the Monarch had teeth now! This was one thing she was qualified to do. 'Suppose I clean your teeth while I explain about the procedures?'

'Excellent.' He settled on the throne and opened his mouth. His teeth were surprisingly similar to those of a human being: twenty four of them, divided into incisors and molars, sixteen and eight respectively. No cuspids. Normal occlusion. That, as galatic dentition went, was practically, identical to her own set.

She brought out her instruments, set up the sterilizer, and tied a protective cloth about his furry neck. This was awkward, because his head was not attached in a familiar manner, but she had learned not to let such details interfere. She lifted a scaler and began to check.

'Your teeth are not in the best condition, I'm afraid,' she remarked. 'There's a good deal of erosion, and the gums—'

'Ouch!'

'Are a trifle tender. You need the attention of a dentist.'

'Allow a *moth* to touch my royal teeth?' he demanded incredulously.

Oh-oh. 'Don't you have any butterfly dentists?'

'Certainly not. No butterfly would soil his dignity by learning a trade.'

'Trade? Dentistry is a *profession*.'

'*Kingship* is a profession, my dear. I would have any subject who fell so low as to practise a manual art put under the lights.'

'The lights?'

'Executed, to employ a euphemism. You would not care to know the details, my charming alien hygienist.' Then he fathomed her thought. 'No, there is no such restriction on aliens; we understand that the ways of the galaxy differ from ours peculiarly. No stigma attaches to *you*. You are not at fault for having been hatched on a barbarian world.'

That did not allay all her concerns, but she let it pass. Judy was beginning to appreciate the full extent of the problem. No wonder the Monarch had lost all his teeth.

'Well, I can show you how to extend the life of your teeth, but it's already pretty late. Too much damage has already been done.'

'Ten years is not far enough back?'

'I'm sorry, Your Majesty, it isn't.'

'Explain anyway.'

She continued to work, cleaning away the immediate residue of what appeared to be years of neglect. 'Oral prophylaxis is much more than just cleaning the teeth. The whole mouth, the entire habitat has to be considered. The food of primitive species tends to be hard, tough and gritty, and it cleans the teeth naturally. But civilized foods tend to be soft and sticky, and many essential nutrients are refined out. And sugar – processed saccharine – well, it's best to stay away from it, if you value your teeth.'

'But I love sweet foods!'

'Your teeth have already informed me of that. If you insist on eating sweets, at least keep your teeth clean at all times. A truly clean tooth cannot decay. And it is important to disturb the natural bacteria in your mouth regularly, for some of these attack the enamel of your teeth. You can't eliminate *all* bacteria, but you can rout them out and keep them uncomfortable, so that they never have a chance to multiply and mass against your teeth.'

'You are beginning to make sense,' the Monarch said. 'But how do I keep them clean?'

'You brush them, for one thing.' She brought out a toothbrush, one of the few remaining from her original supply. Well, when they were gone, they were gone. 'I'm sure you have better instruments and better systems at Lepidop, but the principle is constant: *get them clean*. Now I'll demonstrate the best way to clean off the surfaces, then you can do it yourself after every meal.'

'But—'

It was her turn to divine his thought. 'This can't be considered manual labour. It's *hygiene*. Only the most finicky and enlightened persons practise it. Clean teeth are a mark of, er, nobility.'

'Naturally,' he replied, having known it all the time.

'But brushing isn't enough.' She brought out a spool of dental tape. 'This is more difficult but more important. You have to pass the tape *between* your teeth, like this—'

'Ouch!'

'Now that didn't hurt, Your Majesty! You just expected it to. You pass it between your teeth and pull it back and forth a little, and it polishes the surfaces the brush can't reach. Darn these inexperienced adolescent fingers of mine! There. And right there, in the crevices between the teeth, is where food is most likely to collect, and where the undisturbed bacteria will feed and multiply in their own contented microcosm. You no more want to ignore these places than you want to ignore an assassin in your palace. Bacteria *are* assassins to your teeth.'

'Suddenly I understand you very well! Give me that tape!'

His digits were much stronger than they had been when he was old. Before long he became proficient in both brushing and taping.

'Now,' he said, 'I begin to weary. Take my hand.'

She took it, thinking he needed help, but as the vertigo passed over her she realized that they were jumping forward again in time.

She was twenty-six again, her clothing fitted snugly, and the Monarch was back at forty-two/eighty-odd. His wings were bleached, his antennae sagged.

'But look,' he gasped before she left. 'Teeth!'

He was right. They were so dilapidated as to be almost useless, but they were there and they seemed clean. 'You took care of them!' she cried, delighted.

'For ten (breath) long years.' He flopped on the throne, exhausted. 'Dismissed.'

It was several days before the Monarch summoned her again. 'It is very tiring, revisiting the past,' he explained. 'And tedious, following your instructions. But it saved my teeth for five years longer than they lasted before. You gave good advice.'

'I tried to,' she said, but the whole business amazed her. How could they really have travelled back in time? But if they hadn't, how had the Monarch recovered his teeth? They were not good teeth, but they were genuine.

'Ten years were not enough to grant me perfect dentures,' he said. 'Would twenty years do it?'

Twenty years were equivalent to forty in his life, she remembered. He would be half his present age – hardly past his prime. 'It might.'

'Take my hand.'

She obeyed while protesting. 'But your Majesty. The strain—'

The dizziness overcame her, worse than before.

When she regained equilibrium, things had changed drastically. The Monarch was tremendous – twice his original size – and the throne had expanded to match. His wings were brilliant orange delicately veined, bordered on the fringes with a double row of white spots set in black. His torso was full and strong, his antennae were long and firm. He was a splendid figure of an insect.

And his teeth, as he smiled, were fine and even. He had done it : he had taken them back to the time before dietary dissipation and dental neglect had damaged his teeth irreparably.

But Judy was in trouble. She looked at herself. Her clothing hung upon her in gross festoons, her shoes were like boxes, and her dental case was impossibly heavy.

She had lost two decades. Physically, she was six years old.

'Come fly with me, my dear,' the Monarch said. 'This is my time of power.'

'But I'm not *dressed* !' she wailed.

'Neither am I. Does it matter?'

What use to debate with a butterfly about clothing ! Her blouse was now as big on her as a dress, and far less neatly shaped. She belted it around her middle with a strand of dental tape and discarded much of the rest of her apparel. It would have to do.

They went to the parapet, its outer bulge now swollen into a large balcony. 'But you said equipment wouldn't work for you here,' she protested, remembering what he had said ten years later (three or four days ago, subjective time). 'How can you fly?'

'You jest, my dear,' he said benignly, and hooked four hands into the back of her blouse-dress. She screeched as the dental tape snapped and she had to scramble to avoid complete *déshabillé*.

The Monarch flexed his handsome wings. Air blasted down, and then they were aloft. By the time she managed to knot her outfit securely about her, the palace had fallen away and the ground was already awesomely far below.

Now she was glad she weighed so little. Her blouse was good nylon, but . . .

'Material power,' the Monarch said as they flew. 'It has been claimed by sages on my world and perhaps even on yours that this can not bring happiness, but assuredly it can. At this moment in the span of my reign I control seventy systems, each with one or more habitable planets, and I hold a virtual monopoly on the distribution of Ra radium throughout the galaxy. I have phenomenal wealth, and even the lowliest of my subjects live in ease. Look there?'

She peered as he swooped low. There was a silver city with minarets and flying buttresses, each structure bedecked with scores of bright green butterflies. It was as beautiful a municipality as she had ever seen.

'Is this your capital?' she asked.

He laughed resoundingly. 'This is Luna – the slum-city of Lepidop. Every occupant is a moth. See the ugly spots on those wings.'

The spots were not ugly to her. 'Luna moths,' she murmured.

'And look there!' he said, moving on.

It was a forest, but like none she had known on Earth. Each huge tree was barrel-shaped, its foliage on the outside, its fruit hanging inside. She learned that when the fruit became ripe it dropped so that more could be grown on the same stem. There was preservative gas within the hollow centre, so that the tree gradually filled with its own fresh fruit, a natural storehouse. There was enough stockpiled in this one forest to feed several cities for months.

'And there!'

Now they came upon an ocean of water-colour-paint water. Geysers plumed from its sparkling depths into the sky, forming ambient vapour-scapes of every lovely hue. Swallow-tails spun within these falling mists, spraying rainbows from their wings.

'This is my empire,' the Monarch said. 'This is power, this is beauty, this is joy.' And Judy had to agree.

They returned to the palace. 'Why don't you build a dental clinic in this time,' she inquired, 'so that no citizen needs to have lived without proper care : The best food is wasted if your teeth are poor, and no one can be happy when he has a toothache.'

'What I do now can only affect myself,' he reminded her. 'And you, to a lesser extent. But in our normal time I shall build a clinic for the future.'

She checked his teeth. 'There is some damage, but I'm sure that proper care will preserve these for the rest of your life,' she said. 'Brush them after every meal, and brush the rest of your mouth too, to disturb the bacteria. Use the dental tape, don't eat any more processed carbohydrates than you really have to, and have your mouth checked every six months.'

'But who will do the checking?'

That moth problem again ! And of course the Monarch could not summon any off-world dentist to work on his teeth, in this flashback status. 'I suppose you'll just have to do the best you can by yourself. That isn't ideal, but it will certainly help.'

Then she cleaned his teeth carefully, though her tiny six-year-old hands were clumsy at so specialized a task. She reviewed him on the techniques of dental prophylaxis until she was satisfied that he knew exactly what to do.

Finally they returned to the present. There was some awkwardness about her tangled clothing that amused the Monarch, but he was too fatigued to laugh long. He collapsed almost immediately, frightening her. Twenty years seemed to have been a terrific strain on his system.

The Monarch was old again, but did seem to be in better health than before, as though his attention to diet had helped more than his teeth. And his teeth *were* improved; he was still able to chew most foods without discomfort.

If human beings had the ability to impart their knowledge to their younger selves, as the Monarch had done, they might all have superior teeth, she thought wistfully.

Months passed. Judy was well treated at the palace, and from time to time (figuratively) the Monarch summoned her for conversation. He was inordinately proud of his preserved teeth, and gave her full credit for the advice that had in effect restored them. But her service to him had ended; she could leave Lepidop at any time she found somewhere better to go.

Yet there was a certain lingering dissatisfaction. His teeth were *not* perfect, and she knew that he concealed occasional pains, not wanting to admit this flaw in the gift. It would have been so much better for him to have had the regular supervision of a dentist (even a moth dentist!), for the patient simply could not do everything for himself.

She was increasingly nervous, too, because she had not heard from the University. Trach was long gone and she had no idea how to reach him. She might have placed an interplanetary call, but this was expensive and she did not have a planet to reach. He could be anywhere in the galaxy.

Had the dinosaur notified those authorities of her whereabouts? *Had* they in turn notified Dr. Dillingham? *Had* he been interested enough to put in a requisition for her, or whatever it was at this level? She had supposed that Dr. Dillingham had been satisfied with her performance, back on Earth, and might like to have her as his assistant again. But as a University administrator he would rate the best, and she could not delude herself about her status there. She was used to his mannerisms and individual techniques, and that was all.

She made use of the comprehensive Lepidop library of dental information, studying the configurations of the dentures of a thousand alien species. She visited the lowly moth dentists, and found them a good deal more knowledgeable than the opinion of the butterflies suggested. She asked the translator about the university – its procedures and hierarchy. She waited.

Nothing. Either the message had not got through, or Dillingham was not interested. She was helpless.

'I have had a taste of better health,' the Monarch said, shaking his faintly orange wings. 'It incites me to desire more. If twenty years did this, what might thirty do?'

That would be equivalent to sixty, by her scale. He would in effect be twenty – at the very prime of life. Of course, nothing short of a complete overhaul from the moment of conception on would provide him with absolutely perfect teeth, but—

'If I begin caring for my teeth in the flush of my youth, at the time I first emerged from the chrysalis, they will remain strong forever!' he cried.

She kept forgetting that the butterfly life-cycle differed from her own. Perhaps that *was* time enough.

'Come, my dear – take my hand.'

She tried to stop herself, but his word compelled her just as though she were a butterfly subject. 'Wait!' she cried, suddenly realizing what thirty years would mean to *her*. 'I *can't* go back to—'

And the vertigo overcame her.

It was much worse than before. She felt as though she were being turned inside out through the mouth and dipped in lye. She felt, she fought, she expired, she emerged into—

Nightmare.

The choking crying bleeding miasma of extinction. Her arms were bound in mummy wrappings, her eyeballs were rotten. She screamed with the soundlessness of an anguished ghost. Maggots were feeding on her tongue, flames on her wings.

She had tried to go back to four years before she had been born.

But it was not her own demise she experienced. The Monarch was dead. His ancient husk of a body dangled from her hand when she stood, and when she tried to let go his desiccated appendage it fell apart.

'Murderous alien!' the purple court butterflies cried, discovering her in her guilt. 'You made the Monarch attempt the impossible. You crucified him on your short life-span, and he is four years defunct, and now the Empire will fall!'

Judy found no way to protest. She *had* led him on to it, however unwittingly.

'You shall die the death of a thousand lights!' they screamed. 'Moths shall spit on your remains!'

They put her with all her possessions in a cocoon tower near the apex of the castle. She could see beyond the strands to overlook the lovely countryside, but she could not break the tough webbing or force it apart in order to escape. It was like invisibly barbed wire. In any event, it was a long, long fall to the moat, and sharklike beetle larvae cruised that dreary channel.

Butterflies swooped from the sky, their wings translucent in the sun. Each carried a beamer pointed towards Judy's prison. Some of these rods were silver, some black, some green - all the hues of Lepidop. The insects zoomed at her in single file, and from each weapon a narrow light speared into her cage.

At first she flung herself aside, trying to avoid the profusions of beams, but she could not escape them all. Then she discovered that they did not hurt her. They were merely lights, that illuminated her prison momentarily and faded harmlessly.

Was the execution, then, a bluff?

Pain blossomed in her leg. One of those lights was a laser!

An hour and several scorches later she figured it out. At irregular intervals a butterfly would approach carrying an orange rod – the colour matching the wings of the dead Monarch. This was the laser – the beam she had to avoid.

But it was nervous work. She had to watch every butterfly, and there were always several in sight. The beamers were not easy to see until almost within effective range, so she had only a moment to spot the orange one and dodge its pencil-thin sword of heat. The web-flung bars of the cage inhibited her view at critical moments, too. The beams were somehow set to have effect only in her vicinity; they passed through the cage strands harmlessly, and dissipated beyond the cocoon. She was the only target; when her attention lapsed, she got stung.

So far the wounds had been painful but not critical. Eventually a laser would be sure to strike an eye or some other vital spot, and then. . . .

The death of a thousand lights. She understood it now. A hundred thousand threats, one thousand actual attacks. One or two strikes she could forget; ten or twenty she could suffer through; one or two hundred she could survive with proper medical attention. But a thousand would surely finish her. Those she managed to avoid still took their toll, for she could not relax at any time while watching for them, and sleep would be impossible.

Sometimes one laser followed another consecutively. Sometimes half an hour passed between shots, though the innocent-light butterflies swooped past steadily at intervals of five to ten seconds. The average laser came around fifteen minutes. That would be four an hour, she calculated feverishly, or almost a hundred in a twenty-four hour span.

It would take ten days for the torture to expend itself. Far longer than she could remain alert. Eventually she would sink into unconsciousness, from fatigue if not from wounds.

The death of a thousand lights.

Her eyes ached. The constantly oncoming butterflies blurred. They no longer seemed beautiful; they were wings of horror. Always one passing close, its light aiming, stabbing. Always one a few seconds behind, its beamer lost in the distance. And others, trailing back into the sky – an ominous parade of beating wings.

She cried out. She had nodded off without realizing it, hypnotized by the steadily cruising, flexing wings. A laser had scored, singeing a strand of her hair and scorching one shoulder. It was as though a white hot poker had been jammed against her, destroying flesh and bone to a depth of a quarter inch and cauterizing its own wound.

Night came, but no relief. Now the moths were marshalled to the task, their rods softly glowing in the same array of colours. This was no favour to her, she knew. She had to be given a *chance* to spot the orange ones. Otherwise her vigil would be useless, and she would have simply to lie down and let the beams come. That would remove half the torture and shorten its duration.

She nodded off again, and was struck again – but this time she had been fortunate enough to pick up almost thirty minutes of sleep. That enabled her to remain alert for several more hours.

Then the blurring resumed, and would not be denied. She had a tightening headache, and she knew that the long dismal end was coming. She would waste herself away, fighting it, but her point of no-hope was incipient. All she had wanted to do was to rejoin Dr. Dillingham; the cruellest part of it all was his failure to respond. He *would* have responded, she was sure now, had he been told. Maybe the University had buried the message as crackpot. Maybe he already had a thoroughly competent galactic assistant. . . .

She chided herself for feeling sorry for herself, then reacted angrily: now was the best of all times to feel sorry for herself!

A larger light showed in the distance. She thought it was the rising Lepidop sun, and marvelled that the night should have passed so quickly. But it seemed to be star-shaped. And not natural. With an effort she unblurred enough to make out the glint of metal. A machine of some sort, flying through the air, but no aeroplane!

From it a searchlight-sized beam emerged, sweeping across the planet. Was this the final laser?

She screamed involuntarily as the huge light found her and bathed her blindingly, but she did not burn. The machine came down its headlight as though it were an Earthly locomotive. She could make out no detail of its shape.

Her cage exploded. She felt herself falling, still blinded. She heard the chitter of untranslated moth protests. Something hard caught her arm and hauled her up roughly.

'None but I shall do him die!' a metal voice boomed. Now she knew she was hallucinating, for translators could not fly. 'And thou willst join him there.'

'I know that!' she snapped hysterically. 'At least give me some butter for these little burns. . . .'

And that was strange, for she was not the hysterical type. She wondered when the end would come.

CHAPTER EIGHT

'Doctor, you need an assistant,' Oyster said. He had retracted almost entirely into his shell for an executive snooze, but the ubiquitous translators picked up his watery mumble and spewed it forth full-volume in English.

An assistant? Dillingham had already come to that conclusion. He sat behind such a towering mound of paperwork that he could not properly attend to his duties. In fact, he could not always even remember his official title correctly, with so much else cluttering his mind. At any moment he could be popped off to some simple assignment that invariably turned out to be murderously complex in detail.

Actually, no paper was involved. But computerized busywork and multilingual red tape amounted to the same thing. Every tiny plastic card, of the thousands on his desk, represented some problem of some student that he had to rectify in some manner. Yes, he needed help on the interminable details of his office. He had had no assistant since leaving Earth, and he had never fully adapted to that lack. How he wished *he* could take a mid-session snooze, as Oyster was doing now!

Oyster's assistant was Miss Tarantula, a marvel of arachnid efficiency. In the office or the operatory, at the University or in the field, her eight arms seemed to tie up every loose thread before it appeared. It was because of her that Oyster's desk was clear, and Dillingham realized jealously that if he had an assistant even half as competent his own desk would soon be relieved of its burden. Yet she tended to make him nervous, despite his efforts to repress his Earthly prejudices. She was not *really* a man-sized spider. . . .

Oyster poked an antenna out of his shell. 'Set up a series

of interviews for a prospective assistant,' he said to her. 'Land-going, aesthetic, competent, unattached females—'

'The first is waiting in the anteroom,' Miss Tarantula said. That was the way she was: anticipatory. 'If Dr. Dillingham cares to interview her now—'

'But there's no point in merely talking with her,' Dillingham protested. 'I have field assignments as well as office routine. I have to know how she functions in a variety of situations, particularly under stress. If—'

'Naturally,' Miss Tarantula said. 'You are scheduled to make a promotional tour of planet Hobgoblin today. She will accompany you on a trial basis.'

'But that's not a stress situation. A routine visit—'

'The director also wishes you to investigate certain complaints of a sensitive nature.'

So now it came out. Debating points with Miss Tarantula was futile. The slightest twitch of her hairy front leg brought the web tight. And Oyster himself was no slouch at making things routinely impossible; he seemed to feel that this was good practice for the Directorship. Certain complaints of a sensitive nature? That meant that half a mis-step could result in a lynching!

Except for the Jann. The huge robot's meticulous guardianship was not entirely welcome, but was a fact of Dillingham's new life. If there were trouble on Hobgoblin. . . .

Dillingham felt a headache coming on. 'All right. Brief her and—'

'All taken care of, Doctor,' Miss Tarantula said. Naturally. It was not that she was helping Dillingham, for she was hardly concerned with bipedal mammals; it was that her boss had made a directive and she was being efficient.

The door opened. A grotesque mound of warty blubber slid into the office. It drifted to rest before Dillingham, smelling of castor oil. A black orifice gaped. 'So pleased to meet

188

you, Doctor D,' the translator said. 'I am Miss Porkfat, your trial basis assistant.'

Aesthetic, competent, female. . . .

Dillingham had no doubt that by the standards of her own species Miss Porkfat was all of these. And he could not afford to question any of it, lest he betray an un-University prejudice of taste.

'Very good, Miss P,' he said. 'Please arrange passage for three to planet Hobgoblin, and notify the authorities there of our itinerary.'

'Three, Doctor?' Her voice, audible just beneath the translation, was pleasantly modulated, at least.

'Three. The Jann will be coming along.'

She extruded a snail-like eye-stalk. The orb focused on the shining robot. A quiver started there and travelled on down her body before it dampened out. 'Yes, Doctor.' She oozed over to a private-line translator, asked for interplanetary, and began making the arrangements.

Grade A, so far, Dillingham thought as Oyster woke and smiled benignly from inside his shell. The Jann robots were supposed to have become extinct several thousand years ago, but their terrible reputation lingered on in galactic folklore. Miss Porkfat had excellent presence if her only reaction to the sight of a functioning Jann was one eyeball-quiver.

But still she reminded him of infected slug-meat.

The Hobgoblins were surly creatures: short, big-headed, flat-footed, and ugly by humanoid standards. 'What's that Jann doing here?' the customs official demanded in a whine that even the translator caught. 'We don't allow sentient robots on our planet.'

'He – has to travel with me,' Dillingham said. It was complicated to explain.

'He'll stay in the locker, then.' The official gestured to the guards. 'Put this tin in the cooler.'

The squat troopers advanced on the huge metal creature. Dillingham saw trouble coming, but was powerless to circumvent it. The Jann was as deadly a sentient as the galaxy had ever known, and had sworn to protect Dillingham for fifty years. To do that, he had to stay close. Evidently the inhabitants of this planet had little respect for past reputations, or they would never have gone near the Jann.

The uniformed goblins took hold of either arm. They were barely able to reach up that far, and looked like squat children beside a stern parent. They tugged.

That was all. The Jann did not budge or take overt note of them. Fortunately.

Dillingham and Miss Porkfat completed their business at customs and left. The Jann followed, nonchalantly dragging along the two guards. After a while they let go.

So much for protocol. Dillingham sighed with relief that the robot had not lost his metal temper.

The Hobgoblin Office of Dentistry was imposing enough, externally. But inside the fine large building were distressingly backward facilities. This planet still used mechanical drills, X-rays, and needle-injected anaesthetics. Ouch!

A harried goblin technician galloped up. 'What do you want? We don't allow visitors in here. Particularly not aliens.'

'This is the representative from the University of Dentistry,' Miss Porkfat said dulcetly. The nearest translator was down the hall a distance, so conversation was remote. 'On a promotional tour. Your office was informed.'

'I don't need any off-world tub of lard to tell me what we've been informed! Come back next week; we're busy now.'

Miss Porkfat turned to Dillingham, her eye-stalk quivering again. 'They prefer that we return next week, Doctor D.'

Something about this exchange rankled. 'I heard, Miss P. But this was cleared with the authorities before we arrived, and my schedule does not permit a postponement.' Some promotion!

'We're very sorry, but it will have to be today,' she informed the technician.

'Go fry your posterior!'

'I really think—'

'I'll handle it, Miss P,' Dillingham said, his ire rising. He was not a temperamental man, but his position did not allow him to tolerate very much such insolence. Miss Porkfat was being gentle when she should have been firm.

'You don't have confidence in me!' she cried, beginning to quiver all over.

'It isn't that, Miss P—'

'Why *should* he, blubbertub?' the goblin demanded.

'I'm only trying to—' she began, turning pink. On her, this was impressive.

'Of course,' Dillingham said diplomatically. 'But in this case—'

'Will you creeps get out of here?'

'NO!' Dillingham shouted at the ugly face.

Miss Porkfat began to dissolve. Literally.

'I think this position is unsuitable for you, Miss P,' Dillingham said with as much compassion as he was able to muster in the circumstance. 'If you wish to return to the University and seek an on-campus placement—'

She sucked herself together somewhat. 'Thank you, Doctor D.'

'Good riddance, stinky,' the goblin said, with as much compassion as *he* could muster.

Dillingham walked haughtily by him, though privately

he suspected that the goblin was right. This was no job for an assistant who melted in the face of conflict with abrasive personalities.

'Watch where you're going, stupid!' the goblin screamed. 'I said no visitors. I'll clobber you!'

That was his mistake. The Jann, silent until now, boomed into animation. 'None but I shall do him die – forty-nine years, five months, thirteen days hence, Earthtime,' it proclaimed. By the time the words ceased reverberating, the goblin was gone, thoroughly cowed.

A non-native was waiting in the next alcove. Willowy, sweet-smelling, with a cluster of slender blue tentacles and four soft purple eyes: quite aesthetic, in a surrealistic way.

'Doctor Dillingham? I was sent by the University to assist you on a trial basis. I am Miss Anemone.'

So Miss Tarantula had anticipated his problem with Miss Porkfat! Such comprehension was frightening.

'Very good,' he said. Then, thinking ahead: 'This is a Jann. He's travelling with us.'

'I observed him. A handsome specimen. I hadn't been aware they made robots of that calibre any more.'

No loss of control there! Dillingham glanced down the hall. 'And approaching us is another native technician.'

The Hobgoblin wore a badge of rank that distinguished him as an entity of moderate authority. 'No visitors permitted. Leave at once.'

Miss Anemone braced him squarely. 'This is the Assistant Director of the University School of—'

'Don't waste my time with your ridiculous apologies,' the goblin said brusquely. 'Just get out.'

'If you will check our approved itinerary—'

'One side, sea-spook.' The goblin shouldered by her, intent on Dillingham. He did not get far. 'Ouch!'

'Oh dear me, I'm so sorry,' she said solicitously. 'Did my

spines hurt you? I hope you will report to the infirmary right away. I certainly wouldn't want the toxin to get into your system.' She led the way on down the hall while the goblin rushed off, rubbing his shoulder.

So far, so good. Miss Anemone was not unduly sensitive to abuse, or helpless before it.

They arrived at the main demonstration room. Here the wonders of modern Hobgoblin dentistry were displayed: quaint metal restorations, classic plastic dentures, primitive colour X-ray photographs. Dillingham viewed them politely, then approached the goblin in charge and began his presentation. 'I believe the University can enhance aspects of your procedure—'

'Who asked it to?'

Dillingham was not free to mention the several tourists who had complained to the University. That was the unofficial part of his tour. The described symptoms had been vague and diverse, so that no consistent pattern had developed, and no complainer had actually reported for a University re-check. Thus there was no solid evidence that Hobgoblian dentistry was at fault – just a statistical suspicion.

The kind of thing that had to be investigated unobtrusively, for planet Hobgoblin was sensitive about alien criticism. Unlikely as that might seem, from Dillingham's immediate experience.

'Perhaps a demonstration of technique—' he suggested.

'Oh, so the marvellous University desk jocky wishes to show the outworld peons how to practise!'

Dillingham ignored this. 'We might take a look at some of your problem patients.' *The kind that complain to the University!* he thought eagerly. 'Naturally, if I can demonstrate the advantages of University training—'

'Training, schmaining! If we had your finances, we could

afford a multi-species dontic analyser too, and have instant diagnosis of every—'

'You are correct in your implication that the analyser is one of our more important diagnostic tools. But since it is far too expensive for the average facility, we stress the raw ability of the individual dentist using local equipment. It is the talent that remains after the—'

But the goblin did not let him repeat the maxim he had learned so arduously from Oyster. 'You claim you can use my equipment – and do a better job than I can?'

Since courtesy did not seem to accomplish much here, Dillingham yielded to temptation and abandoned it. Unwisely. 'Yes. And so could any University graduate.'

The goblin swelled with rage – then made an unholy smile. 'You're on, Doc.'

He was, indeed, on. In half an hour Dillingham was ensconced in a model unit set up on a stage in an amphitheatre. Miss Anemone had a desk a few paces apart, and the Jann had a separate booth where he could watch for Dillingham's safety without obstructing the view of the audience. Goblin spectators, every one a qualified dentist, filled the hall.

This was more than Dillingham had bargained on, and he made a mental note never again to speak precipitously. Meanwhile he had to follow through. Somehow things always did become complicated. He was almost getting used to it.

'The prosthodontic genius from Galactic U will now demonstrate how to handle a problem case,' the chief dental goblin announced grandly. 'Pay close attention so you can learn how stupid you are.'

Almost every grotesque little face mirrored the chief's resentment. No doubt of it: University prestige was on the line. If he failed here, there would be severe repercussions. He could, in fact, be eased out of the very position he was in training for: the Directorship of the School of Prosthodontics. The goblins were striking not at him, but at his career – a blow the Jann could not foil. All because of one intemperate remark.

The first patient mounted the stage: a quadrupedal and vaguely equine creature with colourful bird-like plumage.

Miss Anemone intercepted it. 'May I have your name and planet of origin, please?'

'Horsefeathers of Clovenhoof,' the creature neighed, showing tremendous yellow teeth.

'Please describe your complaint.'

'My teeth hurt.'

There was a murmur of nasty appreciation from the audience. Hobgoblin's finest practitioners were present, and Dillingham was sure that every one of them had had this problem: the unspecific response. Miss Anemone, of course, would not let it stand at that. She would question the patient gently but firmly, clarifying and isolating his symptoms until she had a fair notion of his real complaint. That was a major part of the duties of a galactic dental assistant: to get at the facts before the patient saw the dentist, thereby promoting office efficiency.

'Dr. Dillingham will see you now,' she said.

There was a chorus of chuckles and a few hoots from the audience. They knew she had goofed. Well, he could not afford to correct her now. That would only make it worse. He would have to question the patient himself – and make sure never to get into such a situation again with an unfamiliar assistant.

It probably was not her fault. Some dentists preferred to handle virtually everything themselves, and some assistants were trained to honour this. Probably she would have questioned the patient further had he asked her to do so. But Dillingham was far too busy to break in an assistant in all the little ways that were sure to turn up. Miss Anemone would not do.

Horsefeathers ambled over and bestrode the dental chair, opening his long large mouth. His breath was not sweet.

'Can you localize the area of sensitivity?' Dillingham inquired, beginning a routine check with the probe.

'Huh?'

'Where does it hurt?'

'They all hurt. It changes,' Horsefeathers said.

Another appreciative goblin chuckle. Dillingham began to fear that they had thrown him a chronic complainer – one who would object no matter how well off his teeth were.

'I see you have had extensive prosthodontic restoration,' Dillingham observed. Indeed, the mouth was a mass of gold.

'Huh?'

'Lot of work done on you.'

'Yes. All right here on Hobgoblin. Lousy job.'

Silence from the gallery. Dillingham suppressed a smile. 'On the contrary. My visual inspection suggests that this work is quite competent. However, I shall take X-rays to be sure there is no underlying problem.' He tapped a tooth, finding it firm. 'Miss Anemone—'

Another evil gallery chuckle. He looked up.

Miss Anemone was gone. A man-sized centipede occupied her desk. 'I am Miss Thousandlegs, your new assistant. Miss Anemone was called away.'

In the middle of a demonstration? This was getting too efficient! How had Miss Tarantula known?

He also noted with surprise that the Jann was gone. The booth was empty and there was no familiar glint of robot metal. But he was sure the huge entity was in the vicinity – and would be, for the next forty-nine-plus years.

All he said was: 'Please take a full set of X-rays on this patient.'

Miss Thousandlegs rippled over, elevated her forepart, and positioned machine and plates. She was good at it, he had to admit, considering that she had probably only had experience with such equipment in some class on Antique Apparatus. In a moment she had the pictures.

He almost gaped. 'Root canal therapy on every tooth!'

'They were pretty far gone,' Horsefeathers admitted.

They must have been. Root canal therapy was only called for when the central nerve of the tooth became contaminated. Then this nerve had to be removed, and silver or gutta-percha or some galactic equivalent substituted, so that no further decay could occur. It was an expensive process, but it generally saved the tooth. The tooth was insensitive thereafter, of course. Without its nerve it could not feel heat or cold, pressure or pain.

'I see no evidence of decay,' Dillingham said, inspecting the X-rays carefully.

'They still hurt,' Horsefeathers said stoutly.

With no nerves at all, they hurt. Dillingham controlled a sigh, knowing that the dentists of Hobgoblin were enjoying this hugely.

'Do you wish me to check the occlusion?' Miss Thousandlegs inquired.

Bless her! 'By all means.'

She brought a wax plate and had the patient bite down on it so that his teeth imprinted the material in a horseshoe pattern, above and below. She studied this. 'Serious malocclusion, Doctor,' she announced.

Dillingham could tell by the silence around him that the goblins had forgotten to make this test – just as he himself had almost forgotten, in his preoccupation with the impression he was making. Miss Thousandlegs had saved him. It was beginning to look as though he had found his assistant.

'This will not hurt,' he told Horsefeathers as he prepared

his rotary unit. 'In fact, I will not have to use any anaesthetic. I am merely going to grind down some of the surfaces a little. To adjust the occlusion, so that your teeth will meet properly when you bite.'

'But it doesn't hurt where I bite ! It hurts deep inside !'

'This is typical,' Dillingham assured him. 'You see, when the occlusion is imperfect – when your teeth meet unevenly – unnatural stress is placed on certain sections. Portions that are too high are driven back or shoved sideways. While this effect is too small for you to notice ordinarily, it continues to irritate the periodontal membrane – the lining surrounding the roots of your teeth – crushing and bruising it. This lining is tough, for it is there to cushion the impact of constant chewing – but under abnormal stress it eventually becomes inflamed. And then you hurt – deep inside.'

Horsefeathers gazed at him in wonder. 'I never knew that !'

'Perhaps your dentist did not feel this was necessary for you to know,' Dillingham said gently. 'Many patients are not interested in such technical details.' *Until their teeth hurt,* he thought wryly

But the silence of the hall as he worked suggested that the point had been made. It was always best to let the patient know as much as feasible about his condition. An ignorant patient could be a difficult one. Horsefeathers had not been an idle complainer; he had really had pain, though the cause was subtle and slow to develop. His occlusion had been adjusted properly at the time of the massive restoration, Dillingham was certain. But with time and use it had changed marginally, and the jaw had felt the stress. Horsefeathers probably consumed enormous quantities of roughage and spent many hours a day chewing it, so this accentuated the condition.

Dillingham had shown the dentists of Hobgoblin how to

practise their profession – using their own tools. The University reputation would profit. There should be a number of student applications from Hobgoblin next term.

He finished, and flushed the polished surfaces. 'Expectorate, please.'

'Huh?'

'Spit.' The translator was being too literal, rendering a complex word in English into a complex equivalent in Clovenhoofian. But he'd have to tone down his language. 'Now it will be a while before the inflammation subsides,' he warned Horsefeathers. 'But there should be a steady improvement now, until you feel no pain at all.'

'It'll still hurt?' The patient looked dubious.

'It has to heal. When you – when you break a leg, you don't expect it to be good as new the moment the vet sets it, do you?'

Horsefeathers thought about that. He looked at his leg. He smiled. 'Thank you, thank you, Doctor!' he exclaimed at last. 'I'm so glad you came here.' He trotted off, limping a little before remembering that it was his mouth that hurt.

Another patient mounted the stage. This was a native Hobgoblin. Dillingham knew that meant trouble. He had counted his dental chickens too soon!

'May I have your name, sir?' Miss Thousandlegs inquired.

'Go fly a kite!'

True to form, Dillingham thought. And how would she react – by melting or stinging?

'How do you spell that, please?'

Dillingham liked her better all the time. Spelling via translator was devious and suspect, but she had fielded the insult nicely.

'G O,' the goblin spelled. 'F L Y. The A is an initial for Algernon. Last name is K I T E.'

Dillingham reminded himself not to jump to conclusions.

'And what is your problem?' Miss Thousandlegs inquired.

'This tooth – it squishes. Sometimes.'

'May I look at it?'

'You're not the dentist, bugface!'

'Nevertheless, I may be able to narrow down the possibilities and save both you and Dr. Dillingham trouble.'

Grudgingly he let her look. 'Another restoration,' she murmured. 'Tooth appears to be healthy.'

'It's not healthy, stupid. It squishes. Sometimes.'

'Could you show me?'

G. F. A. Kite bit down, almost nipping several of her hair-fine legs. 'Nope. It's not squishing right now. But it does. Sometimes.'

'I'll take an X-ray,' she said. She did.

'When do I see the damn dentist?'

'In just a moment. Let me check your occlusion first.' She did. 'You may see him now.'

She accompanied the patient to Dillingham's operatory. 'X-ray shows nothing but the tooth is mobile,' she said. 'The occlusion is slightly off.'

Kite made a face. 'I heard that about Horsefeathers. But mine is only one tooth and it doesn't hurt, it squishes. Sometimes.'

'Nevertheless, occlusion seems to be indicated,' Miss Thousandlegs said. 'Two plus two equals four. I'm sure if we adjust that, your symptom will fade.'

Dillingham agreed with her – but felt she was going too far. She was not merely getting the facts, she was diagnosing and advising the patient – and that was normally the dentist's prerogative. *He* should add two and two and get four.

He checked the teeth. They were similar to human dentures, and most had been restored metallically. All were solid, including the squisher, except for that trace mobility his assistant had noted.

He inspected the X-ray photograph. She was correct there too. the only shadows in the picture conformed to the restorative work present. It had to be the occlusion, again.

He made the necessary adjustments. But one thing nagged him. The occlusion was only marginally skew. Presuming that this condition had developed only recently, the described symptom was too sharp, too localized.

Two plus two might equal four – but so did one plus three. And the goblin audience was suspiciously silent.

But what else . . . ?

He took the probe and checked around the tooth again. It remained firm, and the gum line was stable. He looked at the X-ray once more. The metal of the restoration shadowed it, one projection extending along the distal surface adjacent to the next tooth. No trouble there.

Two plus two . . .

Interesting coincidence that the Hobgoblin chief should send him two occlusion problems in a row. He would have expected something more devious.

He poked the tip of the probe between the two teeth, verifying that the metal of each restoration touched there. The space was narrow; there was no way he could reach it except by forcing the wire point down, causing the patient momentary discomfort—

'Ouch !' Kite yelped, jumping.

The probe broke through into something soft.

'Equals four !' Dillingham cried. He had found it ! A thin cavity just under the metal, concealed from direct view by its location and the overhanging restoration. Its shadow in the X-ray had been hidden by the configuration of the metal itself. Truly, an invisible deterioration – that squished. Sometimes.

Miss Thousandlegs had almost led him astray by her too-ready diagnosis. Had he corrected the occlusion and sent the patient home, the decay could have continued for months. By the time it received proper attention, the tooth could have been lost. All because the primary symptom seemed to match the wrong condition.

Two plus two *did* equal four. But that was not the whole story.

And the devilish goblin dental chief must have known it – setting the University representative up with a valid occlusion case first. Then the *seeming* occlusion case . . . what a trap!

'Anaesthetic,' Dillingham said. He had had a close call.

Miss Thousandlegs brought the loaded needle. He injected the flinching patient. Oops – it had been so long since he'd used anything this primitive that he'd forgotten to apply a surface anaesthetic before giving the shot, and his assistant hadn't reminded him. Not her fault; she just wasn't familiar with his procedures, his little lapses.

He readied the drill. 'Vacuum,' he said.

Miss Thousandlegs applied the vacuum, sucking the saliva and moisture left from the water-cooled drill.

'Other side,' he murmured, as her instrument obstructed his view. He began cutting away the overhang of the tooth.

He finished and removed the drill. 'Mallet,' he said, picking up the chisel. She held it up, but his hand missed contact. The mallet bounced off his fingers and fell to the floor. The goblins guffawed.

Dillingham's ears were burning. Again – not her fault, he reminded himself. She just wasn't adjusted to his gestures. But it was inconvenient and embarrassing, particularly on stage.

He knocked off the metal crown, exposing the decay. He fished for the gold chunk before the patient could choke on it – and banged into one of his assistant's insect-like arms. She had been reaching for it also.

Dillingham stopped and counted to ten mentally. Miss Thousandlegs was competent and co-operative – but it just wasn't working out. He could not operate effectively with her.

'Miss—' he started. And blinked. Miss Thousandlegs was gone. She had been replaced by a humanoid biped.

He was tired of this long-distance sleight-of-hand. Miss Tarantula might enjoy tugging on interplanetary threads and hanging his assistants in mid-operation, but he did not. 'Vacuum,' he said abruptly, taking up the drill again.

Assistant number four, the biped, applied the vacuum. Her arms terminated in quintuple, jointed digits that pinched together to hold the tube. He had seen more effective appendages for this work, but at least she did not get in his way or obstruct his vision.

He finished his excavation. 'Hydrocolloid,' he snapped. This assistant would have to stand on her own couple of feet; he was out of patience.

She already had the metal form and cold water ready for the hydrocolloid impression. He made the cast without difficulty, and she took it away. He put a temporary covering over the tooth.

'A new restoration will have to be made,' he told Kite. 'I have prepared the tooth and taken an impression, but it will be some time before the restoration is ready. Your local prosthodontists are perfectly capable of doing it, and I commend you to their services. You were quite correct about your problem, and fortunately we have diagnosed it in time to save the tooth.'

'Doctor,' the new assistant said.

'What?' He was tired, and there was something strange about the way she spoke.

'Will you check the other restorations now?'

'The other—' He paused. 'You're right! A good restoration does not go wrong without cause. I'll have to have a look.' It was a dismal prospect, but he could not risk the same kind of oversight the local dentists had made.

He hammered off the adjacent cap. It came away easily – too easily. He scraped at the exposed cement. 'Soft,' he muttered. 'No wonder there was trouble.'

The goblin chief was about to be snared in his own prosthodontic trap.

The assistant took the gold cap and cleaned out the debris. Dillingham hammered at the next restoration. This one was stiffer, but finally came off. The binding cement was similarly soft. 'Brother!' he muttered. 'They must all be defective. The cement is deteriorating. Real trouble coming up.'

'Now just a moment,' a voice objected. It was the chief dentist of Hobgoblin. 'I did that work myself. There is nothing wrong with it!'

Dillingham glanced at him tiredly. So this was a personal matter with the goblin now. An excellent opportunity to embarrass the chief before his entire profession, to torpedo his planetary prestige.

He was tempted. The chief had tried to trick him, and had almost succeeded, and the audience had been thirsty for his blood right along. He could get even with the whole species of Hobgoblin and make its dentistry the laughing stock of the galaxy.

He saw that the Jann was back in his booth. That made it safe: he could tell off the planet with impunity, for the huge robot would vaporize anyone who dared attack. There would be blood and carnage and flame—

Dillingham shook himself. What was he thinking of! He was here to make friends for the university, not to incite riot. He *really* needed an assistant, if his nerves were this tight. Someone to cool him off. . . .

'The *work* is excellent,' he said. 'I could not do better

204

myself. The *cement* is defective. Give it time and every res-
oration will come loose. This entire mouth will have to be
re-done. And every case where you used this type of cement.
They are all suspect.'

The goblin dentist looked. He pried off another cap and
saw the condition of the underlying cement. He sagged. 'You
are right, Doctor. It was a new variety – not time-tested, but
with the highest recommendations. We used it on our special
patients – tourists, visitors, persons of note—'

'Not your fault,' Dillingham said graciously, suddenly
seeing the answer to those vague off-planet complaints. That
same highly-touted new cement had been used on all of
them! 'Perhaps there is some quality of the local environment that affects the cement as it is being applied. The University will be happy to run tests for you. It's a shame to
have work this good undermined by something this small.'

'Doctor,' the goblin chief said with surprising politeness,
'you have made your point. University training is beneficial.
We shall act accordingly.'

Somehow this did not seem to be the proper time to confess
that he had almost missed the key cavity – or that only the
timely reminder by his bipedal assistant had prompted him
to perform the routine check that had led to the major discovery.

His assistant – she had been perfect! She had done everything just right without intruding. This was the one he
wanted to keep.

'What is your name and planet?' he asked her as he
finished his preparations on the patient.

'Miss Galland – Earth,' she said.

'Very good, Miss Galland of Earth. I want you to—' He
stopped. He had suddenly realized what was strange about
her voice. *She wasn't speaking through the translator!*
Earth?'

'Yes, Doctor,' she said as she cleaned up the patient's ugly face.

Dillingham straightened up and looked directly at her for the first time. She was a young, aesthetic, female human being.

'Judy!' he exclaimed, amazed. 'Judy Galland – my old assistant!'

'I thought you'd never notice, Doctor,' she said, smiling.

'What are you doing here?'

'Why, I'm assisting you. I thought you knew.'

'I mean, here in the galaxy! I left you on Earth, back when—'

She smiled again, very prettily. 'That's a long story, Doctor. Let's just say that I needed a position, and there was an opening. After that it got complicated. Deep space, and all that. Frankly, your robot rescued me from an unfortunate situation.'

He saw now that there were some ugly marks on her arms, as though she had been burned, and she looked as though she had not slept in days. 'Unfortunate situation' could mean almost anything, short of an execution. She was not the expressive type. But she certainly was competent, and he was extraordinarily glad to have her here.

'The Jann brought you?' he asked, picking up the thread. 'But he was supposed to be protecting me! I thought Miss Taran—'

'None but I shall do thee die!' the Jann boomed from his booth, startling them both and causing a ripple of dismay to pass through the massed goblins. 'But thy skein will be too brief without a proper assistant. I perceived thou couldst not endure even forty years in thy solitary condition, and wouldst not have age and wear compromise the letter of mine oath.'

Judy guided the patient out of the chair. 'So you see, Doctor, two plus two—'

'Equals four!' He gripped her by the arm. 'Come on – let's get out of here before Miss Tarantula sends Number Five. I'll settle for Four.'

'And a married man is far more likely to live to ninety-two,' the Jann observed, rising grandly from the booth. 'Had I but my Janni with me. . . .'

Fortunately Dr. Dillingham was not listening. But the goblin audience was, and catcalls resounded.